"A gruesome take on the coming of age story, *To Offer Her Pleasure* gives us well-drawn and empathetic characters and a compelling evil. Tightly written and fast-paced, Seay wastes no time in snaring her readers with sacrifice and dark promises, kept in the bloodiest way."

— LAUREL HIGHTOWER (*CROSSROADS*, *WHISPERS IN THE DARK*)

TO OFFER HER PLEASURE

ALI SEAY

Copyright © 2021 by Ali Seay, Artists, Weirdpunk Books

First Edition

WP-0013

Print ISBN 978-1-951658-17-5

Cover art by Don Noble

Editing and internal layout/formatting by Sam Richard

Weirdpunk Books logo by Nate Sorenson

Weirdpunk Books

www.weirdpunkbooks.com

ALSO BY ALI SEAY

Go Down Hard (Grindhouse Press)

For Ian and Sydney, you are the only reasons I kept going. Thank you for letting me be your Ma.

CONTENTS

Before	11
Chapter 1	13
Chapter 2	17
Chapter 3	19
Chapter 4	21
Chapter 5	25
Chapter 6	27
Chapter 7	31
Chapter 8	35
Chapter 9	39
Chapter 10	43
Chapter 11	47
Chapter 12	51
Chapter 13	55
Chapter 14	59
Chapter 15	63
Chapter 16	69
Chapter 17	73
Chapter 18	77
Chapter 19	79
Chapter 20	83
Chapter 21	87
Chapter 22	91
Chapter 23	95
Chapter 24	99
Chapter 25	103
Chapter 26	107
Chapter 27	111
Chapter 28	115
Chapter 29	119
Chapter 30	123
Chapter 31	127
Chapter 32	133
Chapter 33	137

Acknowledgments   139
About the Author   141
Content Warning   143
Also from Weirdpunk Books   145

BEFORE

THERE WAS a knock on his door and Ben put down his phone. Something in the tone of it, the weight of it—something. He wasn't quite sure. But his stomach plummeted, and his skin grew cold despite the hiss and whine of forced warm air through his bedroom vent.

He heard a sniffle. That was all, a single sniffle, and somehow, he knew. His world boiled down to a single horrible pinprick of light and existence.

The clock on his wall read twelve after twelve and strangely, he felt that meant something. Although somewhere deep down inside he knew it didn't mean a damn thing.

Nothing did.

Ben did not believe in God. He believed in chaos.

His dad had, though. Believed in God that was. Ben couldn't help but wonder how that was working out for him right now at twelve after twelve on a cold winter Saturday afternoon.

Another knock. A little harder. A single blow to the wood with a bony white knuckle. He could picture her there on the other side, barely holding it together. His mother. A tepid and nervous woman even on the best of days. She'd been worse during his dad's illness.

"Yeah?"

The door swung open and she stood there. Mascara running, skin white, chewing her lower lip nervously.

"Benny?"

His throat closed up. He was fifteen. She only called him Benny when things were bad.

Things were bad, though. They had been for a while. And Ben didn't need his mother to speak to know what had happened.

The battle had been lost.

The cancer had won.

And now all that was left was the aftermath.

Much like one of his games set in the wasteland of an apocalyptic world, Ben felt the foundation of his life crumbling down around him.

He loved his mom, but his dad…he'd been the foundation of the family. The strength.

Now it was all just going to slip away.

CHAPTER 1

June

GONE.

There wasn't a note or any real indication that his mother had left beyond the feel of the house. But when Ben walked in and dropped his keys onto the big blue glass plate on the foyer table, he felt the ring of an empty house. An echo that wasn't normal.

She'd left. With Patrick, probably. Patrick the drunk. Patrick who could match her gin and tonic for gin and tonic. Patrick who called Ben "poor little dead daddy's boy" behind his mother's back. Patrick who'd flicked a cigarette at his head once. Granted, he'd been drunker than drunk, but Ben was a big believer that you didn't do things drunk you weren't inclined to do sober.

Ben had picked it up and flicked it back. When Patrick began to posture, Ben had drawn himself up to his full height—6' 2" to Pat's 5'11"—and said, "Try it. I'm angry enough to hurt you, Patrick."

That had been the last of that. Beyond obnoxious words here and there they'd seemed to agree at that moment to avoid each other.

"Mom?"

His voice bounced back to him. A funhouse effect.

He looked at the plate. Her keys were gone.

Her car was gone from the driveway. It was just a yawning empty strip of macadam in the hot sun.

He couldn't tell just how he knew, but he knew.

Up the steps in the warm hush of the house, he went. He pushed open the door to his parents' bedroom with tented fingers. He walked in, stood just past the threshold, taking it all in. He remembered running in and bouncing on that bed while both his parents were burrowed under the covers. Snow day, birthday, Christmas morning, many an instance of bed bouncing sprang to mind.

His father's laughter rang in his head, and he shook it to clear the memory. It hurt too much.

The AC kicked on making him jump.

"Mom?" he said again. Then he laughed. Pointless. Useless. She was gone. She might be back. But probably not.

He sat on the edge of the bed. Patrick's sneakers were by the nightstand, but his dad's closet was still full of his stuff.

His mother had cried one night after one too many G&Ts that it wasn't that she loved Patrick, it was that she was lonely. And not lonely in a way that Ben could fix.

Ben understood that and willed her not to continue in that vein. Thankfully, she didn't. But he also couldn't help but wonder how she, after seventeen years of marriage, couldn't make it five months without a lover.

"Not for you to worry about," he said aloud.

The late afternoon sun streamed in and painted yellow light like an arrow across his father's closet door. Ben went to it, pushed the accordion door open, pulled the string for the closet light.

All the clothes neatly hung on hangers appeared like a magic trick. Striped shirts, plaid shirts, even some fun and funky Hawaiian shirts. Pants neatly folded over hangers; shorts hung with the pant hangers that had grippy jaws to hold them on.

He squatted down, both knees popping loudly in protest.

Got your old man's joints…

He could hear his dad in his head. He had popcorn joints—as he had called them—too. Hereditary he'd said, but Ben didn't know if that was true.

One pair of standard black low top Chuck Taylors, one pair of red high tops. A pair of black dress shoes, a pair of deck shoes, and a pair of sandals.

He smiled thinking of his dad saying, "Look at all these shoes. Christ, you'd think I was a woman."

He didn't mean anything by it. It was a joke about the fact that his mother had literally ten times the number of shoes.

Something occurred to him, and he pushed back toward the rear of the closet until he found them.

"There you are," he said, grabbing the big white box with both hands and pulling it forward.

He sat there, in the mouth of the gaping closet, and opened the box. Inside were nestled a pair of Doc Martens. Oxblood. Low top. Definitely worn but well-loved and well cared for.

"If you love something take care of it." Practically his father's motto.

All his stuff was always stored away neatly. Put in original packaging if possible. Not left lying around. Polished, repaired, shined, cared for. Whatever it was that an item needed to last, his dad did it.

Ben looked at his mother's side of the room. Shoes strewn about, clothing in a pile, a purse she swore she loved dropped by the small table that held a cordless phone and its base. Her side was always chaos, his dad's always order.

Even in death, his father had it more together.

Ben pulled his sneakers off and slid his feet into his father's shoes. They were worn and comfortable. Scuffed in some places but it gave them character. He tied them and stood.

Like a glove.

The shoes welcomed his feet, hugged them. He imagined he could feel the many miles his father had walked in these shoes as he moved.

"I don't want to fill your shoes," he whispered. "I don't think I ever could. But I want to wear them. It makes me feel better."

CHAPTER 2

"HEY, BEN!" Miss Molly waved to him and he waved back.

It was Wednesday night, trash night. He dragged the metal can to the curb and made sure the kitchen trash was out. Otherwise, it would draw flies.

Other kids his age might have forgotten. Other kids his age might have figured fuck it. But he was the one who made sure the house ran smoothly now. Trash day? Ben was the one who remembered. Recycling day? Ditto.

He was the one who made sure the dishwasher got run and made sure the heat got turned off when the weather warmed and cleaned the AC filter in the summer.

He made sure his mother was taken care of. Her absence wouldn't affect him other than being alone.

Completely.

"How's your mom doing?" She called shielding her eyes against the setting sun with her hand.

He shrugged. "Doing okay. Went on a little trip," he lied. It would delay anyone noticing or reporting him being alone.

"Good for her!" Miss Molly smiled at him, but it didn't touch her eyes.

She'd always liked Ben and Ben suspected she disapproved of Lila Schon's boyfriend and her comings and goings.

He shrugged again. "Hey, I got the house to myself! Can't argue with that."

She gave him a wave and disappeared into the shrouded comfort of her home. The moment it got hot Miss Molly drew her blinds and down they stayed until fall came.

He wandered inside, considered a beer, rejected the idea. It was okay to walk in his father's shoes but no need to follow in his mother's footsteps.

Instead, he ripped the cellophane off a microwave meal and nuked it. He turned on the TV just for the company. Steve Harvey joked with a family in the background as he dug through his mother's desk while waiting for his food to cook.

He found her checkbook. The balance read $3,872.02 and he wondered how long that would last. And how he'd pay the bills after it was gone.

Paying the bills wouldn't be an issue either. He'd helped her all through his dad's illness. Bills and other adult things were always something his dad had taught him as he grew up.

"You can never be too prepared for life, son," he'd whispered.

Ben was glad that had been his viewpoint. Because at 16 he was the closest thing to an adult in this house and now, the only occupant at all.

The microwave beeped and he figured he'd worry about the bills when he had to. For tonight, he was absorbing the fact that his mother was gone.

CHAPTER 3

"BENNY, I know you're probably mad at me…"

He listened, holding his breath he realized. He hadn't answered her call. He'd let it go to voicemail. Now he picked at a rubbery piece of microwaved chicken while listening to his mother's watery drunken voice.

"…I just need some time. Just a week or two. Don't worry. I'm coming back. I *will* be back."

Was she trying to convince him or herself?

Tears stung his eyes and he brushed them away angrily. He would not fucking cry because his mother was a broken and absent excuse for a parent.

"Anyway, I'll be back. Just be a good boy. Take care of yourself. I'll make this up to you, baby. I will. I promise."

Then dead air.

Sure she would. She might come back, he thought. But not until Patrick left or money ran out or she found herself alone. Then she might come back and try to mother him again.

"Too little, too late."

He found a shitty horror movie from the 80s and let it run. It was one of the ones his dad had loved, so bad it was good, he'd said. They'd remade it a few years back but it didn't even come close.

On the screen, the scrawny kid said, "Oh, you're so cool, Brewster!"

Ben repeated it in reflex. It was his dad's favorite line from the movie.

He found himself swallowing repeatedly as his throat grew tight. The urge to cry—shit, the *need* to cry made him angry and he found himself grabbing the black plastic tray of his pathetic dinner and flinging it against the wall.

He stared at the grease spot and the dribble of corn and its juices running down the wall.

"No mother, no dog, nobody. I guess I'll clean it up. Or not."

Ben got up, turned the TV up not off, and went upstairs. It wasn't terribly late, but Ben was terribly tired. He went into his mother's bedroom, found a bottle of cough syrup with codeine, and took a dose.

He wasn't sure why he did it, but what did it matter. Maybe oblivion was what he wanted. He loathed booze, he didn't smoke pot — though, he had in the past. The cough syrup just seemed logical.

"And I don't even have a cough."

He left his mother's bathroom light on and the door cracked. When it was time to get in bed, he left her bedroom door ajar and then his bedroom door cracked.

The ambient light and the murmur of the TV from the first floor gave the illusion of someone else in the house.

He dreamed of his father telling him stories, teaching him how to grill, telling him how to use a saw properly, and waxing poetic about the works of Arthur Machen and Mark Twain.

He woke once in the very darkest of night with the thought that he'd wished he'd listened more when his father talked. When he tried to show him things.

If he'd had known their time would end so soon, he would have.

CHAPTER 4

BEN ATE BREAKFAST ALONE. He watched Miss Molly's dog, Sabrina, run through her backyard and attempt to catch squirrels.

When it was time to figure out his day—school being out of session and all—he hadn't a clue. Were his mother and Patrick here, his day would have revolved around avoiding them until it was time for bed. But since they weren't, the day yawned before him, a blindingly sunny void.

The day's clothes consisted of a pair of basketball shorts and a tee, plus his favorite running shoes. He'd forego the Docs for going out in the summer heat.

He found his baseball cap, pulled it over his too-long hair, opened his mouth to yell out to his mother that he needed a haircut, and promptly snapped his mouth shut. So hard and so fast there was an audible sound.

Snagging his drawstring backpack, he loaded in a bottle of water, a handful of fruit snack packs, a protein bar, and an apple. Then he grabbed his phone and his key.

He didn't want to sit in the empty vault of a house all day. It would be bad for his brain. Too many ghosts. The living and the dead.

※

He'd made it over one great group of rocks in the creek. The grayish-brown humps of them looking like some sleeping beast half burrowed in the creek bed. He'd only made it that far before he heard Michael Rogers yell, "Hey, douchebag!"

Ben froze, recognizing the voice. Not wanting to deal with the kid. Technically, he was a friend, but Ben wasn't feeling much in the mood of entertaining—friends or otherwise.

Much like a stray, though, once Mikey had found you, it was hard to shake him.

Ben tried to keep going. He gave it a good effort. He just kept moving forward, head down, hoping maybe Mikey would assume he had earbuds in or something.

No such luck. He heard the kid coming. He was like a goat. One of those naturally athletic types who could do just about anything that involved sports or natural grace. He was as dumb as one of the rocks Ben was standing on, but he could move like it was effortless.

Within seconds he was standing there, barely breathing hard, grinning. His phone in his hand, his earbuds dangling around his neck, his big eyes covered by skiing sunglasses no doubt stolen from his red neck of a dad.

"Hey, man."

"Hey, Mikey."

"Mike," Mikey corrected. "Mikey is for babies. My birthday is next week."

"Sixteen?"

The kid nodded. "Yep. You already turned right?"

"January." Ben kept walking, hoping that maybe he could magically slip into another dimension and walk alone and think, which had been his intention.

Mikey stayed right on his heels. "Where you going?"

"Nowhere."

"Cool. I come out here all the time. My house butts up to the hill up there. I can get to the woods or the cemetery whenever I want. It's good for when my parents go at it."

"Fight?"

He shrugged. "Fighting. Fucking. Usually, one or the other."

"Eew," Ben said before he could stop himself.

Mikey just laughed. "Yeah. Eew."

"So where are we going?" He asked after three whole seconds of silence.

"*I* was going for a hike."

Mikey paused and Ben kept walking. "Am I bothering you, man?"

"Does it matter?"

He sounded shitty and he wasn't a fan, but God, it had been a suck ass 24 hours.

"Well, yeah."

Ben blew out a breath and tried to get his head on right. It didn't sound like Mikey had it any better than he had at home.

He kept walking. "If you want to come, come. If you don't, don't," he yelled over his shoulder.

There was a single beat of hesitation and then Mikey's shoes pounded in a steady cadence behind him. Then he was at Ben's side, hands in his cargo short's pockets, grinning.

"So where are we going?"

Ben shrugged. "Wherever this path leads."

Ben could only take care of listening to so much about the other girls teasing Karen Jackson about her gigantic tits and whether or not he thought the school nurse put out on dates or not. He had no idea that Mikey was such a gossip.

The truth was, Ben didn't care much about girls because no girls interested him. Not beyond the girls in his D&D Club – Alice Day to be specific – and somehow, messing with any of them seemed like a bad idea.

Don't shit where you eat...

One of his father's favorite sayings. He'd always understood it. He loved D&D Club when school was in session. He didn't want to ruin it by liking a girl and then something going wrong. Even if it was how he truly felt.

"—gotten laid?"

Ben looked up from the mud. He'd been tracing patterns in the wet soil with a stick. He saw his father's initials, a half-moon, a lightning bolt, a star, a fucked up smiley face, and a bunch of lines. "What?"

"Have you gotten laid?" Mikey said overly slow like there was something wrong with Ben.

"Nah. Not yet. I'm not really worried about it, to be honest."

"You're not one of those…" Mikey twirled his finger in the air trying to conjure the world.

"Fag?" Ben drew the word out, assuming that was what he was going to hear and hating it.

Mikey's eyes widened. "No. And you shouldn't use that word, man. Not cool."

Heat flooded Ben's face and the irony made him laugh. "I only said it because I thought you were going to and then *I* was going to call *you* on it."

Mikey shook his head. "Thanks for the vote of confidence."

Ben laughed again. "Sorry. Bad assumption. So, what were you going to say?"

"The people who don't have any interest in anyone."

"Asexual?"

"Yeah, that," Mikey said.

"Nah. Just haven't done it yet, that's all. No biggie."

They got up and kept walking. For a while they were silent. Ben wondered if Mikey was the kind that needed to know he was accepted before he could be around someone in silence.

They turned up at a very overgrown bit of the path. This part hadn't been used very often. Ben paused, wondering if they should turn around. Instead, he pressed forward. He wanted to see what was at the end of the trail.

At this point, he had nothing to lose.

CHAPTER 5

"Jesus, it's like something out of a fairy tale," Mikey said.

Ben just stood there looking and marveling. It stood in a small clearing amidst the towering skinny trees. A small weather-beaten shack that looked like it was held together with spit and bubble gum – another dad-ism.

Mikey, apparently possessing absolutely no fear or common sense, walked right up to the haunted shack and grabbed the handle.

"Maybe not," Ben said.

Mikey shrugged as if to say what the hell and yanked. The door came open with a blood-curdling squeal. Then a sudden voice barked, "Who's there?"

Mikey froze. "Hello? Is someone here?"

"Of course I'm here. It's my motherfucking house." Then the sound of boots thudding across a wooden floor.

Ben took off and Mikey was close on his tail. Laughing. They ran back down the path and dodged to the right taking a smaller spot that was barely more than a minor crushed line in vegetation.

"Jesus Christ," Mikey said.

Ben dropped to a fallen log to catch his breath. He didn't say anything because he was breathing so damn hard, but those boot thuds sounded like they were coming from a far back room, or possibly even down the steps from a second level.

Which was impossible. The shack appeared no more than two rooms wide. If that.

What was the hearing equivalent of an optical illusion? An audible illusion? The Doppler effect?

"—and like eat us for fucking dinner!" Mikey said on a high donkeyish laugh.

Ben didn't ask for the missing sentiment. He simply nodded and said, "That was weird." Then: "I have to get home, man. I'll see you."

"You don't want to…hang out a bit more?" Mikey looked disappointed and a little worried. About going home? About being alone?

"Maybe later. I have some stuff to take care of."

"For your mom?"

Everyone knew his dad was dead. He was the dead dad kid.

"Yeah."

In reality, their run in with the Hansel and Gretel shack in the woods had put his mind to his dad's vast collection of old books. One of them was a book of fairy tales.

The real ones, boy. Not the Disney version. These will put the hair on the back of your neck up.

And he suddenly wanted to be surrounded by those books, his dad's stuff, memories. If he'd known, he'd have listened better.

Mikey was still talking when he turned suddenly and started walking.

He was relieved when the boy didn't follow.

CHAPTER 6

A COUGH ERUPTED FROM HIM. A cherry-scented cough that tasted like someone had set a cherry tree on fire. He nearly dropped his father's pipe but managed to pluck it from the air, the bowl so hot he fumbled it again.

"Fuck!" he said. Then promptly coughed until he thought he'd throw up.

Somewhere in the distance of the humid night, thunder rumbled. When he was little he'd been afraid of storms. Until his dad had taken him out on the porch one night and they'd sat in the dark, just the two of them, watching, "the light show." That's what his father had called it.

Every time the thunder would rumble his dad would cheer. Every time the rain blew on them his deep baritone laugh would fill Ben's head. Storms stopped being something to fear and became a spectacle to be enjoyed.

It would be nice to go out and watch when it hit.

Ben put the pipe in an oversized glass ashtray to let it burn out and cool off. He sat in the middle of the basement room in an old gold high-back chair that was probably way older than even his mother and looked at the walls and walls of bookshelves.

He couldn't find the fairytale book. But he knew if he kept looking he'd find it. He'd found a lot of books on war, some on medicine, some on gardening.

His father had known a lot about a few things and a little about a lot of things. He never tired of learning and Ben had kind of picked up on that. So, when he spotted the golden tomes, four of them, that were roughly the same dirty goldenrod color of this father's reading chair, he got up and went to them.

All four were by an author named Arthur Machen, and way back in his memory he recalled hearing his father say the name. Encouraging Ben to give him a try one day. His father had always cheered reading anything—everything. Better to be over-educated than under.

The books were clothbound, discolored, with green patterned inside papers. The pages were deckled and yellowish and the heft of them felt good in his hands. Maybe he'd give them a try.

He flipped one open. *The House of Souls*. Inside was an index listing four stories. One of them was *The Great God Pan*. That also rang a dim and tinny bell in his mind.

He'd read them, he decided.

"What else do I have to do, right?"

He wondered if he could get a dog now that his mother was gone. At least he could talk to it. That would be nice.

Thunder boomed so loud and so sudden, it made him jump. He dropped the stack of books and they splayed out at his feet.

"Shit."

He crouched, gathering them up. A spricket jumped from its camouflaged state and made him jump again.

"Fucking thing!"

The basements in this area always had the damn things. Looked like some cross-breed of a cricket and a spider, they were supposedly blind and could hop like motherfuckers.

He wasn't a bug fan.

Ben stood and caught a flash of dim red at the way back of the bookshelf.

Crouching, he looked in the space where the four yellow books had been. There was definitely something shoved back there.

After setting the Machen carefully in the chair, he pulled two books from the left of the hole and two from the right. All four were antique slim volumes he hadn't examined yet.

He'd get to those later.

Maybe this was the missing fairy tale book. Would make sense why he couldn't find it. He slid his hand back in the hole and got ahold of the book. About the size of an old-fashioned memory album, the kind you glued the photos into. It was soft clothbound, worn smooth in spots and discolored in others.

He looked at the cover and found an embossed line of flowers and leaves and random designs but no title. The spine held no title either.

It took him flipping four pages into the book to find a title page.

To Offer Her Pleasure

No author.

The fine hairs on the back of his neck tingled. Outside lighting strobed, its cold light shining briefly in the high narrow basement window.

Thunder rumbled and he went upstairs, holding the book. The Machen forgotten on his father's reading seat.

CHAPTER 7

IN THE CONTINUED vibe of channeling his father, Ben decided to try his port wine. He found the tiny glasses his father kept for the fortified beverage and rinsed it in the sink. He gave it a quick dry with a paper towel and poured the dark red liquid into the bell-shaped glass.

It wasn't very impressive. A weak-ass amount of red wine is what it looked like to him, but he figured he'd see what it was all about. The TV rambled on, a different game show filling the room with chatter.

Ben drank down half the port in a swig. Which was a good idea because it tasted like hot ass. He opened the book and looked at it. The words seemed to swim and sway.

He flipped until he found an illustration of a robed figure with horns standing in a flowering field. Despite the flowers which would indicate day, the shadows and sky looked like night.

Something about the trim but imposing person made him feel uneasy.

He tried again to read something and the words wouldn't behave.

"Can't be drunk," he said, shutting the book. "Must just be tired and sunblind."

At the mention of sun, the AC kicked on as if it knew the muggy night was pressing in on the small house.

He turned the light off but left the TV running. He stuck his key in his pocket and left the book on the living room table. Then went out on the porch, sank into one of the aged Adirondack chairs, and watched the sky light up. He smelled the ozone, listened to the angry giant rumble of thunder, and drank the rest of the port.

The heat of the June night and the heat of the wine worked through him. His cheeks felt like they were glowing in the dark.

He picked at the hem of his shorts and said aloud, "I miss you. I don't so much miss her. I miss you, though. Once you were gone, she checked out. More interest in the bottom of a bottle than in me. And then that asshole Patrick came along and—"

He put the tiny glass on the small table between the chairs, sank lower, and watched the heavens.

Wind blew back his hair and brought the fresh smell of rain-drenched grass to him. He shut his eyes for a few minutes and when he began to doze, realized how crappy his sleep had been the night before.

His mind played the movie of Mikey traipsing through the wood chattering non-stop. The weird little haunted-looking cabin. The voice, the thundering bootsteps coming from a structure too small for any running to be accomplished. The smell of his father's books, the basement smell, and finally, stuttering like an old reel-to-reel film, the jumpy image of the figure in the book.

It moved. It walked. It swayed. Long hair rippling. Turning, it was turning, and the horns moved elegantly. A single arm came up to point his way as the figure—she?—kept turning and turning. And turning forever. It never seemed to face him.

Something brushed his leg and he sat up straight hissing "shit" between pursed lips. Slapping at his leg. Rubbing like he'd been burned.

It touched him again and his brain allowed him, this time, to process the sensation. Soft. Damp.

Followed quickly by a soft meow. He exhaled loudly.

A cat. A god damn cat.

He looked at it and said, "You're not a cat at all. You're a *kitten*. Where did you come from?"

He scooped it up just as lightning struck way too close. "Right. Inside we go," Ben said, and carried the cat—a girl cat—inside the house.

He shut the door against the storm and went about finding a can of tuna and a bowl for water.

He woke twice in the night. Once when the cat climbed onto his chest and nestled just beneath his chin. The second time, she was purring so loudly it vibrated him into consciousness.

He thought about moving her but decided to let her be. She'd had a rough night. So had he. It couldn't hurt.

Solace was good for everyone his father had once told him.

Solace.

"Solace," he whispered, and stroked her once before drifting back off.

At least he was no longer alone in the world.

CHAPTER 8

HE WAS EATING a piece of toast and an apple when someone came banging on the door.

The cat darted off into the dining room and he had to laugh to see her scamper.

He'd tried again to read the book he'd found in the basement, but no such luck. Ben was starting to wonder if it was actually in English or just one of those languages that looked readable until you tried.

Some of his father's books had fooled him before.

He hadn't intentionally revisited the illustration of the figure but found himself staring at it when the banging started.

Walking as softly to the door as he could, he quietly pressed his eye to the peephole. At first it was dark, whoever it was, was standing too close. Then they stepped back, and he exhaled loudly when he saw Mikey Rogers big fucking goofy face right in front of the door.

"Jesus—"

There was a moment where he nearly walked away, but it wasn't good to hide alone when everyone in his life was gone. That was right, wasn't it? Being an introvert was one thing. Being cut off from everyone and rejecting any attempt at friendship was unhealthy.

He wanted to be healthy. He wanted to be brave. He wanted to be normal.

Ben unlocked the door and unhooked the chain. He opened it slowly and tried on a smile. It felt stiff and awkward.

"Hey," he said.

"Hey, man. I wanted to know if you wanted to go walking again. That was pretty cool. My folks…they woke up going at it today and I'm not in the mood. Figured I'd see if you—" He shrugged, looking suddenly unsure of himself. "Were interested in tagging along," he finished lamely.

"I have to do a few things. But I can meet you there in an hour," he said. "Mouth of the trail."

Mikey's face lit up and it made Ben sad to see that the boy was more excited than he was. This kid had a family and couldn't wait to get away from them.

"Cool. I'll see you then."

Ben agreed that he would and shut the door. He sat down in the cool silence and went back to the book.

For a split second he saw a word or two that his brain could read. Flesh? Blood?

Then back to gibberish.

"Dad, you were a weirdo," he said.

He went and found another can of tuna, making a mental note that he'd have to grab more soon.

Solace came running the moment she heard the can opener. Didn't take her long to catch on.

He put the tuna down and gave her fresh water. There was a box in the pantry and Ben fished a newspaper out of the recycling. He shredded the paper as best he could, set it in the box, and hoped she'd take the hint to use it as a bathroom until he could get a litter box.

"Be good. Use your potty. I'll be back later," he whispered.

As he walked the mile to the park, he wondered why he was hanging out with Mikey. He had no interest in being social. No need for a friend. He simply followed his intuition and that was to agree.

There wasn't anything better to do, really, beyond find a litter box for Solace and maybe some cat food.

Mikey was waiting in the parking lot at the top of the trails. He was bouncing from foot to foot like a drug addict awaiting his next score.

"You okay?" Ben asked. He dug a bottle of water out of his back-pack and handed it to the boy.

Mikey's face lit up like Ben had given him a Christmas gift.

"Yeah. My parents. They are…" He rolled his hand in the air. "Nuts. Nothing. It's fine. Just thought another walk might be fun. Yesterday a crazy shack, maybe today a troll under a bridge."

He snorted and Ben smiled.

"You never know."

CHAPTER 9

THEY DIDN'T FIND a bridge or a troll. They did find something odd.

"What is it?"

They'd walked a good forty-five minutes until the trail became overgrown. The area they landed in was a wide-open space dotted with lumps and holes.

"A hole," Mike said, shoving his head down in it.

They weren't straight down holes but appeared to go into the ground at an angle.

"I know it's a fucking hole, idiot," Ben said.

Mikey laughed, his head still in the empty space, so it echoed.

"I don't know," Mikey said aloud and Ben could hear his voice traveling. Riding away but then echoing back.

The boy pulled his head out and surveyed the swayback landscape. "Fucking strange." Then before Ben could say a word, Mikey dove headfirst into the hole.

Ben's heart seized in his chest. He actually grabbed his pec like he was having a heart attack. He dropped his water bottle on top of his backpack and raced to the yawning disc of darkness.

"Jesus fucking Christ! Mikey!" No answer. "Mikey!"

"It's Mike!" Mikey said but he simply sounded far away.

There was a sharp whistle that caused Ben to look up. From all the way on the far side of the clearing, Mikey waved.

"How—?" Ben muttered under his breath.

As if he'd heard, Mikey gave him an enormous grin and yelled, "Tunnels! They're fucking tunnels! Come over."

"No way!" Ben said.

Who knew how they'd gotten there. Who knew if they'd cave in.

Again, as if reading his mind, Mikey yelled, "They have struts. Or…what do you call thems? To hold it up. No cave-ins. You'll be fine. Too low to walk but not low enough that you have to crawl. Just ya know—crouch!"

Ben considered just walking away but he decided what the hell. It was the middle of a blazing hot day and he had nowhere else to be and no one waiting for him. It didn't matter one way or the other.

Ben put his backpack on and ducked down. He entered the hole much more slowly than Mikey had. Once inside, he saw that distant light coming through the tunnel. He walked, stooped over like an ancient man. Here and there, the tunnel branched off to others. The light shining from them as well. It was dark in the tunnel but not pitch black. He had very little trouble maneuvering.

Within a few minutes he reached the end, emerging into the startling light where Mikey waited, laughing.

"Is this fucking cool or what?" he shouted, fist-pumping the sky.

"Or what," Ben said, but found that he was grinning too. "I wonder why they're here. What the hell they're for."

Mikey shrugged. "Who knows. Who cares? They're fun. We should see if we can get over there." He pointed to the far side where a sole Birch tree stood. Gangly and skinny in comparison to the rest of the trees, mostly Oaks.

He took off like a rabbit. Darting into the tunnel, laughing as he went.

After a minute Ben followed.

They managed to traverse all of them. The final one was a bit rough. As if whoever's handiwork this was had run low on energy or time.

Mikey was ahead, yammering about how they could turn them into secret hiding places. Or a very long clubhouse. He suddenly hissed and said, "Dammit!"

"What's wrong?" Ben wasn't very interested at that point, but it was the right thing to say.

"I caught my shorts on a nail or something sharp. Tore 'em."

"You okay?"

"I think. I scratched myself. A little blood. I'm fine." And then Mikey, like any foolhardy boy who has very little fear, was off again.

Ben paused when he found the spot. Two indentations in the soft earth from Mikey's knees. A small nail poking out of the wooden bone works that braced the tunnels. A small scrap of fabric clung to one. The worn khaki from Mikey's cargo shorts.

When he touched it, his hand came away wet. Blood.

He could smell it then.

Something deep inside Ben exhaled greedily.

Murmuring to him to take the treasure.

He did. Plucking it from the nail like some odd cloth fruit and pushing it into the front pocket of his shorts.

He hurried toward Mikey's ever-present chatter and emerged into the bright light of day.

CHAPTER 10

THE CAT HAD USED the litter box. Then she had playfully spread the shredded newspaper all over the kitchen floor.

Ben exhaled and ran a hand through his drenched hair. He was beat. Hours of hunching his way through tunnels and then the walk back to the mouth of the park and then the hike home had left him sweaty and wiped.

The cool darkness of his house was welcome. And so was the silence.

Mikey never stopped talking.

"Well, you sort of did what I asked," he said.

The kitten rubbed against his ankle and meowed. He glanced at the clock. Five thirty almost.

"Hungry?"

That seemed to be the magic word. She curled around his ankles like smoke.

He found a can of chicken breast and gave her the whole shebang. He still needed to get her food.

For a moment, he watched her eat and then grabbed a banana from the bowl. A swarm of fruit flies erupted when he disturbed them, and he realized most of the fruit was past ripe and headed swiftly into rotten.

He picked up the bowl and dumped the remainder in the garbage. Then he tied off the bag and took it out to the garage. After dumping it all in the can, Ben stopped.

"Ah ha!" he said, looking up.

On the single long thin shelf that ran along the right side of the garage was a bag of kitty litter. His father used it when the weather got bad to get traction under the car tires should they get stuck.

He looked beneath the workbench and plucked out a sturdy aluminum turkey pan. His dad had always saved those after Thanksgiving dinner because they were "good to have in the workroom. A million uses!"

He never threw out anything he thought he could use, and at the moment Ben was supremely grateful for that.

He now had a proper makeshift litter box for Solace.

Inside, he set it up, washed his hands, and made himself a Lean Cuisine. They always left him starving, but it was one of the few frozen meals his mother would keep on hand.

He followed it with two store-bought brownies and a protein bar. All that tunnel crawling had left him starving.

His new companion followed him into the bathroom while he showered. She was batting something around the floor when he got out.

Ben wrapped a towel around his waist and snagged her prize from her.

It was the bloody scrap of fabric. He'd forgotten about it.

Ben had a sudden and intense moment of vertigo, like someone had tilted the floor, but then it righted. He put the bloody bit of cloth on the windowsill and said, "Find something else. That's mine."

He'd sat down in front of a cooking show to eat some chips but then the first fork of lighting outside lit the living room in a flash. Followed quickly by a rumble of thunder, Ben found himself staring at the book. This time the form of the figure (woman?) was turned a little more toward him, he thought. A curve of a cheek visible maybe.

The antlers were at a slightly different angle from what he remembered.

Solace pounced on his big toe and chewed it with her little needle teeth.

"Ouch!" he said, snapping out of his reverie.

His skin was tingling like the lighting had struck too close, but he thought it was the book. He also noticed his dick was at half-mast. Like he'd licked a light socket.

He gently moved the cat and put her on the back of the sofa to explore.

His head did that buzzy vertigo thing again and he shoved his hand in his pajama pants pocket and found the bloody scrap of fabric he'd left there.

Intuition, stupidity, weird thoughts, too many horror movies—whatever compelled him to do it, he had no idea. He slid the fabric into the book, so it touched the tightest spot where the pages met. He looked at the figure (her?) again and waited.

Then he laughed at himself.

A word flashed then, coming into quick focus before fading back into gibberish letters when he concentrated.

Sacrifice.

Was it his imagination or a trick of the light? Did it matter?

He shut the book, wondering when and if he revisited it tomorrow (he would) would the figure (woman) be more visible to him? Would he see more of the face?

Would the small scrap of garbage he'd pocketed for some unknown reason please it?

Solace jumped onto his shoulder, scaring the shit out of him.

"You're a little fucking lunatic, aren't you?"

He found a sci-fi movie on Netflix, laid down, and let the cat climb all over him.

He was tired. Bone dead tired. But his brain was racing and alert. The storm only amped him up.

His phone notifications informed him, at some point while he'd been spacing out with the book, his mother had called again.

This time she hadn't left a message.

CHAPTER 11

HE STOOD at the breakfast counter with his microwaved breakfast sandwich watching the cat eat.

When the doorbell rang, he looked up into the bright light streaming through the front window.

Mikey?

Probably.

He dropped the other half of the sandwich in the trash on his way to the door. Parts of it were still frozen and he found the whole thing pretty disgusting.

When he looked through the peephole, he was surprised to find Miss Molly's plump face staring back at him.

She smiled at him when he opened the door.

"Hey, Ben. I wanted to check on you. Make sure everything was okay."

He stepped out into the bright light and rising humidity of the day. "Sure. Why wouldn't it be?"

She waved a hand at him and laughed. "You know me, an old busy body who worries too much. I know your mom is on vacation." At that word, her face puckered up like it had before and Ben had to keep from laughing. Miss Molly really did disapprove of his mother. "And we had a power blip last night and those damn—sorry, darn— raccoons were out again last night. Trash everywhere. I just wanted to make sure you were okay."

"I'm okay," he said, shrugging. He hadn't even noticed the power blip or known about the raccoons.

"Good. I know. It's none of my beeswax but I do worry. I've known you since you were a baby. Your dad used to bring you to the fence and I'd give you popsicles in the summer."

He smiled. "I remember."

"Your dad. Such a good, good man. I miss him." Her eyes went wide as if she'd made a faux pas and she hurried on. "I mean, nothing like you do, of course, dear. But he was my friend, I dare say and—who's this!" she said suddenly, clapping her hands together.

Ben jumped at the sudden shift in her train of thought.

He looked down to see Solace peeking out. Her black fur sleek in the bright sunlight.

He reached down and scooped her up. "This is Solace. She showed up during that storm the night before last. I brought her in out of the rain and it looks like she has no intention of leaving."

"Oh, my," Miss Molly cooed, plucking the kitten from his hands. "She is a gorgeous one. Black cats get such a bad reputation for no good reason. Lovely. And with big green eyes. Such a looker. Yes, you are. Yes, you are..." She cradled the kitten.

Then Miss Molly hissed, drawing her hand back.

"God. I'm sorry," Ben said, reaching for the cat.

Miss Molly gave her over with a smile. "Claws. They don't know what to do with them at first. She'll grow into them."

He was alarmed to see a streak of crimson sliding down the older woman's finger.

"Miss Molly, I—"

She waved her good hand at him. "Hazard of being an animal lover. I'm old, dear. I have thin skin. She barely scratched me. Though, I had better go clean this up. You call me if you need anything?"

He promised he would, and she hurried off.

Solace was trying very hard to work something out from beneath her claw. He took her paw and pressed her pad to extend her claws.

Ben removed a very fine sliver of skin from beneath the curve.

"You really did get her."

Solace sniffed the skin flap as he pulled it back.

Inside, he went to the book and opened it. He only had a moment of surprise when he found the perfectly clean scrap of fabric inside. Any traces of blood and dirt that had been there, were gone.

Ben pulled the cotton out and dropped it on the coffee table. Then he slid the thin offering of flesh between the pages.

He had deliberately not looked at the figure (her) in the picture. He wanted to wait.

But he had seen a word swim into lucidity. The word MORE.

He shut the book with a thud and decided to ride his bike down to the small grocery at the end of the cul de sac. It was that or ride the forty minutes to a big chain in town.

"I'm going to get you real food," he said.

The kitten cocked her head, turned on her side, yawned, and fell asleep.

"I can tell you're very excited."

He went to the hutch where his mother stored the good dishes and found what he was looking for tucked inside a big ceramic mug she'd brought at a craft fair. A bank envelope with about three hundred dollars in it.

The money held no excitement for him. He had his own stashed upstairs. If anything, it was a reminder that his mother had simply decided to leave him here to fend for himself. This was her grocery money, kept in the same place since he was small. The only time he'd ever gone there to get money and there hadn't been any, was right after his father had died.

There had been a lot of gin that month and very little food.

He shoved the money in his back pocket, exited to the garage, and headed out.

The sun was blinding, the heat stifling, but he felt the low-level hum of excitement under his skin. He couldn't quite explain it. He knew it had to do with the book and the figure (woman) and the blood and flesh.

It had to do with mystery. With power. With secrets.

A shiver ran up his spine despite the heat and he realized he was grinning. The same way he felt when a big storm was coming. Electric, alive, and a little bit fearful.

CHAPTER 12

MILLARDS WAS at the end of School Road. Once upon a time, it had been a small white house. Now it was a small white corner store.

His mother often shopped here not just for convenience, but their prices were reasonable, and she believed in supporting small businesses. The Millard family lived in a house they'd had built behind the store when they purchased the property.

Ben always parked his bike between the back of the shop and the front of their house. That way it was less likely to get stolen while he was inside.

"Ben!" Mr. Millard yelled.

The old man was starting to stoop, and his glasses got thicker each year. It had been him and Mrs. Millard who'd bought the shop, but now it was his son who ran it. He lived a few streets over.

"Hey there, Mr. Millard. How are you?"

He went to the aisle that had the pet food and found tiny dainty cans of cat food and a big clunky bag of dry food.

"I'm good. How's your mom? Haven't seen her in a bit."

"She's okay. She's on a trip right now."

"That's nice."

Ben nodded, realizing suddenly, that it was. He had things to do and books to figure out.

"Yep."

"And how are you?" Mr. Millard asked, squinting through the leaded glass windows he called glasses.

"Good. Keeping busy."

He put the food on the counter and the old man raised an eyebrow. "Get a new pet?"

"Yep. Little kitten. She's cute. But I don't have any food."

"Now you do!" The old man rang it up, took the money, and then rummaged under the counter for a moment. He put a small mouse made of felt and feathers on top of Ben's bag. "A gift for the newest member of your family."

Ben laughed. "Hey, thanks, Mr. Millard."

The old man waved it off and snorted. "Be careful going home. Did you park your bike around back?"

Ben grabbed the bag off the counter. "Yep. Why? Is that okay?"

"It's fine. Just be careful. Jason's back there and he has a new toy."

Jason Millard was Mr. Millard's son and the man who did most of the running of the store.

"What'd he get?"

"New table saw." The old man winked. "Men love to cut things up."

Ben laughed. The men he'd met did, in fact, enjoy cutting things. Tools in general. Doodads and gadgets.

"I'll keep an eye out."

He talked with the old man for a few more minutes and then there was a far-off rumble.

"Uh oh! Storm's coming. Better get going, kiddo."

Ben hurried out the back door and draped the bag of cans over his handlebars. He was just about to push off when he heard a shout. Then the sound of Mrs. Millard's high wavery voice.

He peeked around the side of the house.

Jason Millard was holding his hand up before his face as if he'd never seen it before. Crimson wetness slipped between his fingers, flowing rapidly from the fresh wound. The tip of his middle finger was gone.

Mrs. Millard was alternately yelling and scanning the ground.

Ben started toward them, his mouth hanging open in shock.

"Don't, don't!" Mrs. Millard said when she saw him. "You don't want to see, Ben. Don't!"

Ben froze, but not before he felt something under his shoe. Something that could totally be a rock. He knew it wasn't. He could feel its give. He could simply *tell*.

Mr. Millard had come rushing out, and worried about Ben being traumatized, no doubt, patted his shoulder as he passed. "Go on home, Ben. No need for you to see this. He'll be fine. It'll be fine."

They were all occupied, so Ben lifted his shoe, bent, and retrieved the fingertip.

Meat and bone glistened. Dirt stuck to the wet blood. It was a gruesome sight. And before he could think about it, he shoved the fingertip in his back pocket.

He rode like the wind to beat the storm.

In the garage, he sat on his bike for a moment. He could feel it. The palpable sense of anticipation.

It was waiting for him.

The book.

The figure (woman).

He knew it.

More.

CHAPTER 13

THE FIRST THING he saw was teeth. Then horns. She turned from where she stood facing the wall in the corner, stepped toward him—

Ben jumped up so fast he fell. He laid there on the floor by the foot of the old gold-colored reading chair in the basement. He'd come down with his father's pipe and Port and had sat trying to commune with the dad that once was.

Somewhere in there, he'd fallen asleep.

He studied the corner where she'd been standing. In his dream.

"Was it a dream?" he whispered. He didn't like the sound of his voice. The fear. The raspy nature.

He got up off the floor.

"Of course, it was. There's the corner. Nothing. Nothing there at all."

His fingertips tingled. It had been so eerie. So fucking real. Like the moments in an otherwise boring horror movie where a jump scare is inserted.

The book.

He'd put the fingertip in the book. The flesh from poor Miss Molly had been missing (eaten). And he put the fingertip in the same spot. Again, he hadn't looked at the illustration of the figure (woman). He'd wait.

He'd put in more and wait.

"Can't put anything much bigger in there," he'd said to Solace, laughing. The fact that he was feeding a book was unnerving. He tried not to think about it.

She'd simply cocked her head at him as he pressed on the book as hard as he could to keep the finger smashed inside the hefty volume.

It had still bulged. It popped open once, but he leaned on it a bit harder. Something cracked. Another noise slipped out. He tried not to think about it.

He also tried not to think about Jason Millard minus his fingertip forever because he stole it for a picture (woman) in a book.

The basement called to him, so he'd made his way down to be with his dad's things, and possibly somehow to connect with his father. Every day—every moment—that passed he missed his mother less. Realized how very little she'd truly meant to him. How little she'd been in his life since his dad died.

Once Patrick came along, he was something to get lost in. She surrendered herself to their relationship. The drinking, the fighting, the making up.

Ben had faded away.

He heard a noise. A soft, sliding, thumping sound from the back room. A makeshift workroom where his dad kept his toolboxes and Christmas decorations.

It sounded again. Stealthy. Secretive.

His body grew tight, but his bowels and bladder loosened up. His skin tingled like there was another storm brewing.

With that came a rumble of thunder, and just below it, that sound again.

He turned on his heels and hurried up the steps. Halfway up, he put on speed feeling like something was right on his heels. About to reach out, snag his foot or ankle, yank him back, and keep him in the darkness.

At the top of the steps, he slammed the door, and turned the lock. Then he promptly tripped over Solace who let out a half shriek half hiss and squirmed so hard beneath his foot he went down on his ass.

Again.

"Jesus fucking Christ!" he cried, feeling like an asshole.

His father had always said that anger was easier than pain or sadness. Anger is an easy emotion.

He was angry.

Under it, he was scared.

The thunder boomed again, the lights flickered, and then they went out.

"Fuck."

He found his phone in his pocket, used the flashlight, and made his way into the living room where he knew there was a big pillar candle in a hurricane lantern on the table.

Also, on the table, was the book. It was open.

CHAPTER 14

THE FINGER WAS GONE. Completely.

Ben tried very hard to look at where the digit had been and not at the page with the illustration (woman). But the figure (she) was waiting for him. Now in profile. Long insane hair, horns that may or may not be attached to the very humanoid head. Her profile was beautiful and frightening.

There was a hint of teeth, then very long teeth, then none. Her eyes faced forward, her eyes looked at him slyly from the corners, her eyes were black discs in her head.

Every time he tried to focus something shifted.

The book seemed to exhale, and Ben fought the urge to drop it.

His eyes, in the dim candlelight, tried desperately to translate what he was seeing. They wanted so badly to read and yet, could not.

More. More.

Moremoremoremoremoremoremoremore

He shut his eyes and shook his head and the book seemed to quiver in his hands.

He'd given it offerings. *Offered her pleasure*—and now, now it was trying to get more.

There was a dry whispering sound deep in the center of his head and then a cold waterfall of fear trickled through his insides.

The storm raged, the tree outside slammed the house, the wind picked up.

The lights and TV and AC all jumped to life at once and Ben screamed. This time he did drop the book.

Solace, who had been sitting there somewhere in the dark, pounced as if he'd just offered her the most enormous new toy. She jumped on the faded-red dirty cover with her two front paws.

Without thinking, he snagged the end of her tail, only wanting to save her. He wouldn't be surprised at all if the book yawned open to swallow down the black bundle of fur.

She didn't like it. Not one bit. Like the compact ball of muscle and claws she was, she reared up and took a chunk out of his finger.

Claws or teeth, he hadn't a clue.

But he was bleeding.

He kept his calm, walked her to the steps, and put her halfway up. Then he swatted her ass gently and she took off like a shot.

Ben went back to the book, let it fall open naturally, refused to look at the siren—the woman—the figure—and smeared his blood in the seam where the pages met.

"There," he said. "Eat up."

He put the book in the middle of the coffee table, blew out the candle, and as an afterthought put the big heavy hurricane lantern on top of the book.

Just in case.

⚜

The pounding woke him and he sat up. A lump of fur slid off his chest and then turned and ran, insulted by the abrupt relocation.

"Sorry," he muttered as the cat took off. He ran a hand over his face, wondering if he'd been dreaming. The pounding had stopped.

His bladder complained and since he was awake, he figured he'd drag himself out of bed and pee. Just as his feet hit the floor, the pounding started again.

There was no way Miss Molly was banging like that. He thought she might even have a key to the house for emergencies. Anything that would cause her to have to bang like that would warrant just coming in.

"Coming!" he shouted, hoping whoever it was would stop the noise.

He pulled on his shorts and a tee and hurried downstairs. The pee would have to wait.

If it was Mikey, he was going to beat him senseless.

He ripped the door open, ready to scold whoever it was, and the words froze on his tongue.

Along with a push of humid heat, came the smell of cucumbers and watermelon. Alice. Alice Day's perfume. It always made him hungry when he sat near her in D&D.

"Hey!" she said, brightly.

"Hey," he said. He took a step back realizing it was morning, he'd just gotten up, he was wearing shorts and he may possibly have an issue.

A hand subtly passed across the front of his shorts alerted him that he was fine.

"Sorry about the banging. But I thought you wouldn't hear if I didn't. I rang the bell a few times, but nothing."

"How did you know I was here?"

She shrugged. "A feeling."

A feeling?

"Did you..." he petered off, not sure of what to do or what to say. *What do you want* seemed rude. He settled on: "Want to come in?"

"Sure," she said, pushing past him. Her hair was cut to her chin in a chaotic mass of chocolate kinks with a few stark blond streaks she must have put in since school ended. Her chin was pointy, her eyes an intense brown, her nose an adorable ski slope. She had a single dark mole near her full lower lip and she smelled like summer.

"Hi," he said and then shook his head. Stupid.

"Do you have the hardback rule book from D&D? No one seems to have it and I was thinking of having a group of people over sometime this summer to play."

"I don't. I thought Steve had it."

She rolled her eyes. "God. I hope not. I don't want to go over there. His mother tries to get me to like him. And I mean, as a friend, he's fine, but not like...that. You know? She's a nosey woman. Tries to play matchmaker. And trust me, that's not going to happen. Do you have any Coke?"

The question threw him off guard and he shook his head as if to clear it. "I—um. . .maybe?"

He headed to the kitchen to check, and she followed. He became very aware that he hadn't brushed his teeth, was wearing an oversized tee for his former middle school that had been his dad's (Go, Tigers!), and had a severe case of bed head.

He opened the fridge. It was depressing in there. Nearly empty. The dregs of milk, his mother's tonic, a browning lime, some old cheese, and a box of baking soda.

That left the pantry.

He side-stepped her, inhaling deeply as he went, sucking in the artificial but bright scent of cucumber and watermelon.

He squatted and saw two cans toward the back on the very bottom shelf. "It's your lucky day," he said, laughing. "Mine, too. There's two of them."

He snagged them and stood, pulling tall glasses and ice out and making their Cokes.

They stood there drinking. Outside, someone was mowing their lawn. Someone else's kid was screaming so loud it sounded like a homicide was being committed.

"Do you want to come?" Alice blurted.

He nearly spit out his mouthful of soda. Somehow, Ben managed to swallow it. "What?"

"To the D&D night? When I have it? Do you want to come?"

"Oh. Yeah. Sure. That'd be great. We haven't played in a while and it's hard to get everyone together in the summer."

She nodded, looking way too serious for her years. "I know. It's sad. But if we do it the first week of July, everyone seems to be okay. You'll be here? Not away on vacation or anything?"

He laughed. "Nope. Not me. No vacation."

She nodded. "Good. Now I just need to find the book."

"I'm pretty sure Steve has it," he said. Then his hormones got the better of him and he said, "I can go ask him if you want."

She brightened. She held out her hand. "Phone?" she said.

He blinked, and then caught on. "Hold on. I'll be right back. I have to get it."

He hurried up to his room, grateful to have a moment. He grabbed his phone, brushed his teeth, peed, and tried his best to stick his hair into place.

Alice Day. In his house. All long legs, big smile, doe eyes, and smart as shit.

He had to psych himself up to go back down. She scared him in the most wonderful way.

CHAPTER 15

SHE KEYED her number in with thin fingers that made him think of artists and piano players.

"Call me when you find out?"

"No problem. I'll bring it here? If you want? I mean…if he has it."

"That'd be great." She looked at him with those pretty eyes and his heart kicked hard like a donkey in his chest.

There was a tickling whisper inside his head. Way deep down. The primal part of him.

His skin broke out in goosebumps.

The book. Whispering way down deep in his brain. It liked Alice.

He didn't like that.

"No worries." He took her arm and tried to hustle her out of the house. He didn't want the book around her. "I have…something to do. But I'll go over as soon as I'm done. I pretty sure he has it."

She closed a hand around his wrist and her cool fingers felt like heaven on his anxiety-heated skin. "And you'll come? To my D&D night?"

"Sure. Yeah. Of course—"

Never had he been more torn. Stand there and let her touch his skin that way. Feel the sensation of her fingertips pressed against the place where his pulse beat or get her out. Just in case.

"I really have to go, Al. I'm sorry."

She smiled. "You're the only person allowed to call me Al."

He opened his mouth, shut it, opened it again. Ben Schon doing his finest impression of a freshly caught bass.

She stood on tiptoe and planted a kiss on his cheek. Simultaneously, his brain shut down, his dick woke up, his heart pounded like a drum, and somewhere in him there was a howling call for blood.

Her blood.

It terrified him.

He smiled. "I feel special. I'll get back to you as soon as I know." He pushed her toward the door. He stepped out onto the porch with her. Then thinking more of it, he walked down the walk with her toward the main sidewalk.

She faced him and he didn't let himself think. He cupped the back of her neck and did what he'd wanted to do for about a year now. He leaned in and kissed her.

She was still for a moment, and in his mind, he started screaming—*Asshole! Asshole! You fucking moron! She didn't want you to kiss her!!!*—but then she kissed him back and he didn't want to die anymore.

When the kiss broke, he took stock. He still felt the call of the book, but it was farther off, distant. He could get away from it—to a degree.

"I'll call you," he said. Then he turned around and headed inside. He needed to see if there was any of his blood left in the margins.

꙳

Steven Browning was a pudgy nosy whiney kind of guy. They all tolerated him fairly well in D&D but outside of the extracurricular he could be trying.

Ben pedaled his bike as fast as he could, wanting to get this over with. The day was very hot, but his skin felt very cool.

There hadn't been any blood in the book where he'd smeared it—fresh or otherwise. No tell-tale brown smear to show that he'd offered it a sip of himself the night before.

The figure (woman) in the picture had turned away from him some as if pouting.

"Well if you want Alice, you'll have to pout," he'd muttered. "I'm not giving you even a taste of her. Not a single one."

He'd slammed the book shut and put the hurricane lantern back on top. Then, as if an extra precautionary measure, he'd put an ashtray from the side table on it. A big marble one his mother used for company.

Not that anyone but her and Patrick still smoked in the god damn house.

Now, out in the beating sun, he wondered if he should burn the book. Just thinking it, though, made his stomach turn like he might throw up. Did he have some link to it now? Some connection that couldn't be broken?

Had he offered it (her) too much pleasure? Too many tastes of what it wanted?

When he'd stared at the book to check for his blood smear, a single word had swum up out of the gibberish on the page.

SURRENDER

He'd shivered then, and he shivered now thinking about it.

Steve's house was a brown two-story with fading wooden shingling, a forest green roof, and deep red trim around the windows. The front door was rounded at the top and painted red to match the trim.

It reminded Ben of a gingerbread house, and Steve the chubby little greedy kid who would try to eat it.

He dropped his bike gently on the lawn and headed up the forest green steps to the wide front porch. He rang the bell and then stood there feeling hot and awkward.

Inside, behind the rounded red door, a TV chattered.

The door popped open and Amanda Browning stood there in her yellow sundress and flip flops. Her screaming pink hair was done up in long braids and she chewed on a piece of gum like she was punishing it.

She was eighteen, two years older than Ben, and looked at him like he was a bug on her shoe.

"Steve! One of your little asshole friends is here."

"Gee, thanks," Ben said, but she was already gone.

Steve came to the door with an ice cream in his hand and half of it was on his shirt. Ben had to fight the urge to roll his eyes.

"What's up, man?"

Steve pushed the screen door open and stepped back. Ben had no choice but to accept the invitation.

Amanda was on the sofa, scrolling on her phone, whatever talk show she was watching—or not watching as it appeared—screaming loud in the background.

Steve was staring at him, waiting.

"Oh, shit. Sorry. I spaced out. I'm here to see if you have the D&D rule book? The hardback? From club?"

Ben nearly cringed. The way he was talking, he sounded like one of the popular girls who always ended every sentence, regardless of what it was, with a verbal question mark.

"The white one?"

Ben thought it was white. He was fairly certain. So he said, "Yeah."

Steve shoved the dripping point of the cone into his mouth, swallowed, and then turned toward the kitchen. Ben could see the stove and the sink from where he stood.

Ben said over his shoulder, "Yeah. I think I have it. Come on."

First, thank god, Steve stopped and washed his hands. He wiped the excess water on the seat of his shorts.

Then he surprised Ben by going out the back door and into the yard. Ben followed.

"What do you need it for?"

He didn't want to give away Alice's party, so he said, "I was thinking of working up a campaign for the beginning of school. A surprise."

"Oh, cool. Can't wait."

Steve was walking toward the back gate. Ben ran to keep up. "Um, where is it? Not in your house, I guess?"

Steve grinned. "I guess I can tell you," he said with a teasing tone.

Who was he kidding? He sounded like someone desperate to share a secret. And for that Ben felt a stab of sadness.

"Go on," he said as they walked out the gate and to the woods beyond. It looked to be a fairly large section of woodland and now Ben was intrigued.

"I have a little...bunker. It was a bunker once. And it's abandoned. I found it about a year ago by accident. I haven't told anyone but my cousin Daniel and he lives in Minnesota so he hasn't even seen it. He said I was making it up. But I'm not. He can get fucked."

That sudden and shining anger was not a surprise to Ben. This was a kid who could one day be on the news for shooting up a large gathering.

There was a lot of buried rage in Steve. Anyone who stopped to look long enough could see it.

Steve moved faster than he'd anticipated. Ben had to race to keep up.

"Sorry. My sister's friend, Kelly is coming over and I want to see what she's wearing. She wears these tank tops, man, that you can look right down the middle. So, when she bends over there's a row of tit on each side, then an empty space, then her belly button, then her short waistband. And ya know, I can only imagine what's beyond that." He rolled his eyes in an exaggerated gross way and Ben had to force a knowing smile onto his face.

"I hear ya," he said.

And unfortunately, he did. But whatever. He was running around town stealing fingertips. Who was he to judge?

They passed a row of young fir trees, a felled oak, an old rusted sign that said, *NO HUNTING PERMITTED!*

"I think the crazy guy who used to live in our house built this thing. Like a bomb shelter. I think he moved into our house in the late 40s and you know the whole nuclear war scare and radiation and shit."

"Sounds cool," Ben said. Because it did. Regardless of his mission, he wouldn't mind seeing a mid-century bunker.

"It is. Underground." Steve laughed at his own joke.

"Why is it out here?"

"What's that?"

"The book? Why is it out here?"

He sighed. "My mother goes through my shit. My dad and sister and grandma, too, but mostly my mom and she thinks that D&D is Satanic. She thinks we're worshipping the devil or some shit."

Ben couldn't help but laugh. It wasn't the first time he'd heard that. Thankfully, his mother had been eyelashes deep in booze and wouldn't have cared if he were actually worshipping the Dark Lord himself.

"Oh, man, sorry about that."

"Eh, it's fine. At least I have this sweet spot to hide all my shit. Nobody knows about it, so I don't have to worry about anyone messing around in it."

Nobody knows about it…

Those words raised the hair on the back of Ben's neck and he did his best to ignore it. That whispering itching tickle deep inside his head took note of the fact that they were going somewhere that no one could track Steve to. Or him, for that matter.

"No," he said aloud, trying to banish the thought.

"What?" Steve slowed and looked over his shoulder.

"Oh, nothing," Ben said, coughing to cover the single word he'd ejected. "Got an allergy cough. Pollen."

"Christ, you too? It's miserable this week? All the yellow jizz all over the cars and stuff. My mother's been trying to pump me full of Benadryl for days."

He started to slow down. "There it is."

Ben looked around. "Where?"

Steve laughed. "Good, isn't it?"

He pushed aside a few overgrown branches, hefted a few huge rocks with grunts and groans, and then kicked some dead leaves aside and there it was. A metal hatch with a busted hasp.

"Wow," Ben said.

CHAPTER 16

AT THE BOTTOM of the swinging emergency ladder, he nearly fell. It was dark and damp and echoey with the sounds of his sneakers hitting the concrete floor.

Steve was already down there. Standing. Waiting.

Ben's heart did a double tap. She was there in the corner of the bunker. Lurking in the dark. A flash of movement. The intimation of teeth, claws, wild eyes, and fury. Her hair a mane that spoke of violence and wind. Then a lovely maiden. Bewitching. Intoxicating. A Fury. A Valkyrie. A Champion. Ben knew what he had to do, and he acted immediately.

He clapped his hands together and used them as a club, hitting Steve on the back of the head. The boy went down to his knees.

"Ben, what—"

Ben hit him again and when the chubby boy fell to his side, he kicked him in the temple. Once. Hard.

Then standing there, horrified and sick to his stomach, he patted his pocket for his phone. He used the flashlight to find one of those battery-operated push lights attached to the wall. Steve had put up a whole row of them and Ben went down the line pushing them so they sprang to life.

On the floor, Steve groaned but didn't try to stand. He was either out, or at the very least semi-conscious. He was most definitely stunned.

He coughed, then coughed again harder, without even opening

his eyes. Something rattled across the concrete floor and Ben trained his light on it.

A tooth. A big one. Blood and root attached.

He reached down, plucked it with two fingers, and turned to the still-murky corner of the bunker. "Is this what you wanted?" he shouted. "Is this good?"

His voice, big and angry and more than a little scared, bounced back at him. A boom loud enough to make his brain hurt.

"What are you making me do?" He screamed it. Unafraid of anyone hearing him beyond the boy he'd just beaten into submission, he let loose his fear and anger.

"Ben? What happened?" Steve was trying very hard to sit up. "Did I fall?"

"Yeah. You fell. Stay down a minute. You're woozy."

Steve obeyed and stayed down, breathing shallowly, blood leaking from the corner of his mouth.

Ben looked up from the boy on the floor and she was there again. Pale, long drawn up mouth, razorlike teeth, haunting eyes that were more the absence of eyes than eyes. Then a hitch in his breathing, a blink, and she was a stunning ray of light. Golden halos around her horns. Her hair. Her trim shoulders. She smiled and he peed his pants.

The glorious horror that was the (figure?) woman in his father's book.

He saw the D&D manual then. Sitting on top of a stack of tits and ass mags no doubt lifted from an adult. He grabbed it and surveyed the bunker. A few lawn chairs, an inflated raft, some pillows, snacks of course, and other miscellaneous shit.

Ben squatted, patted Steve's pockets for his phone. He found it, shoved it in his back pocket, and stood.

"Ben, what are you doing?"

"Going to get you help."

"But my phone—"

"Don't worry about it. I'll be right back."

He went up the ladder with the manual for Alice tucked beneath his arm. He glanced back to see if the woman was there, but she wasn't. No doubt, she was at home waiting for him. In the red cloth book or out of, he didn't know.

At the top of the ladder, he drew it up quickly.

Steve yelled out then, "Ben! What are you doing?"

"Getting help," he lied.

He slammed the hatch and replaced the very big rocks one by one. He was huffing and puffing by the end, so he was fairly sure even if Steve could get up to the hatch, he'd never be able to push it open.

He arranged the camouflage leaves and branches and hurried back to his bike.

The tooth in his pocket felt hot like it was radioactive. It seemed to burn a hole in his pocket.

What did she want? What would she give him? Did he really want to know?

CHAPTER 17

THE BOOK WAS OPEN AGAIN. Sitting there on the coffee table. The hurricane lantern sitting by its side. The ashtray as well. It was as if the book had moved it all and just flipped itself open as easy as you please.

"Hello," he said. He heard how shaky his voice was. He didn't like it, but he understood it.

He fingered the tooth in his pocket. The root still felt wet. The blood was long dry. It was 97 degrees outside and climbing.

The shades were drawn, the AC hissed, and Solace walked in like she owned the place.

She looked at him, hopped up on the table, and sniffed the book.

"Down!" he boomed, startling them both. "Leave it be," he sighed. He lifted her with one hand and dropped her on the sofa.

He had no doubt, given the chance, the book would eat that cat.

"Don't fuck with it."

She gave him a disgusted look and wandered off.

He finally looked. Looked right at the picture. She was in profile. Her brow more pronounced than what had ever been considered pretty. Her horns had wicked curves. There, once again, was the suggestion of predatory teeth and menace. But a glowing kind of presence that made him feel. . .calm. Wanted.

Loved?

He snorted. She wasn't his mother.

She could be…

"No. My mother is gone."

Someone to take care of you. Look out for you. Protect you.

Or have me bring scraps of flesh and bone as offering—

Tit for tat.

There was a loud boom and the TV winked off and the AC died mid wheeze.

A transformer had blown. Happened at least once a summer and practically made him shit his pants every time it happened.

Within moments, there was the siren song of fire engines and cop cars. He wasn't sure of the connection, but it never failed to happen when one blew.

"Shit," he said. "I guess I could leave or..." He didn't want to leave. Didn't want to go out in the heat. He was quite suddenly very very tired. His mind supplying him endless made-up movies of Steve down there in the hole he treasured because no one else knew about it.

No one else knows about it...

He could hang out in the basement. Sit in the atmosphere of his father and be cool in the process. Outside, thunder rumbled. An afternoon storm dying to unleash. It would make the new transformer take longer. BGE would come out, but not until there wasn't a chance of lightning. Fried electrician wasn't their aim.

He flipped the book shut, but not before seeing the word GIVE swim to the surface of the nonsensical words.

"Keep your pants on," Ben said. "You'll get your tooth."

He was taking the book for two reasons. He wanted to keep it in sight, and he didn't want Solace left alone with it. He worried one day the cat he'd managed to rescue would simply disappear. Nothing more than an offering to the horned woman in the pages of his father's book.

In the basement, he lit a row of candles his father kept along the top of a low bookshelf. They were prayer candles from the international aisle in the grocery store.

Andrew was a pragmatic man who believed in being prepared, but also frugal. His mother had always joked that Andrew would pinch a penny until it screamed, but Ben didn't think that was true.

It all depended on what you were spending on.

Candles? Get the cheapest most practical you could.

Books? Get what your heart desired. Get what you needed to read. What your soul craved.

And with that thought, he regarded the book. Leaning back in the ancient goldenrod-colored high back chair.

Rain, insistent and noisy, tapped the low-slung basement windows. He heard the wind like some distant beast on the prowl.

He looked at the inner pages again. TO OFFER HER PLEASURE.

He flipped through the book. Saw words that his brain insisted it recognized but could not read. He rifled through the pages until she showed up.

Her back to him once more.

Pouting until he gave her the tooth?

"What did you do for him? Why would he have this book?"

His father had told him once that the only thing he'd ever really wanted was a family. His own father, not being a stellar guy, and inspired Andrew to want to have a family of his own and treat that family as it deserved. With love and affection. To treasure that family. And make the unit of family mean something—everything.

Ben fished around in his pocket until his fingers found the tooth. He put it in the seam of the book but didn't shut it. He pressed it against the pages. Tried very hard to focus on the words. Willing his eyes to make sense of what he was seeing.

Dizziness slammed him and he swore he saw her twitch right on the page. Gleeful of his efforts? His failure?

A dot of the dried blood was on his fingertips, and he was curious. He smeared it across her image. The page felt hot beneath his fingers. It seemed to vibrate like a plucked guitar string.

He put his fingers over the tooth and shut his eyes but not the book.

He felt a mild spinning sensation like the time his cousin Greg had convinced him to do shots of Southern Comfort and he'd ended up throwing up things he'd eaten the year before. At least it had felt that way at the time.

The sensation passed eventually. He became aware again. The way he did when he lightly dozed off. He came back into himself and opened his eyes.

The blood on her page was gone, the tooth was still trapped beneath his fingers. Her face was turned 2/3 of the way to him and she was smiling. It had a coy effect. But it made goosebumps break out along the tops of his arms.

The rain pelted the house harder. The candles flickered. She looked like she was moving. A Zoetrope effect. He felt nauseous from it.

She turned fully toward him and smiled. Her mouth appeared to reach up way too high. Like a Glasgow smile but healed with scar tissue. Her eyes were enchanting. Tilting up slightly. Exotic. Silver, like polished coins. She moved slightly—or was it the flame flickering?—and her horns lowered just a bit.

There was, a smudge of brown-red across the tip of one. It was wickedly sharp and dangerous looking.

"He's in a hole. I put him there. Because of you, right? What do you want from me and what are you going to give me? Because that's how this always works. Books, fairy tales, horror movies. This is the part where I should stop but I don't. I don't, and everything goes terribly wrong."

He felt her urging him. Silently. Give her the tooth and she would explain.

He felt both elated and sick. Giddy and unsteady. He finally slammed the book cover hard enough for it to echo in the silent room.

He shut his eyes, rested his hands on the old red cover, and waited. He felt himself slipping but he embraced it. Maybe this was all a giant stress hallucination and if he went to sleep—if he surrendered—it would go away.

CHAPTER 18

HIS FATHER WORKED at the bench in the back room. His workroom. His "man cave". He always said it with air quotes.

"I see you over there," he said, not turning his head. He smiled. His fingers moved deftly over the stuff on the workbench. Small comforting noises followed. Metal on metal, wood being shifted, things being sanded.

Ben watched but didn't. He more watched the way his father moved than what he was doing. Like every motion while fixing or making something was second nature.

"Why don't you come all the way in?"

Ben shrugged. He was happy there in the doorway looking.

"Were you poking through my things again?"

Ben thought of the book. He'd been looking at it. Looking through it. It scared him, but excited him, too.

"You need to be careful," his father said, still not looking up. "She gets very hungry. She will give you what you need, but she will take from you too."

What did he need, Ben wondered?

What could she give him?

She was hungry already and he'd done the best he could—within reason —to keep her satisfied.

She scared him deeply.

But he wanted more.

"She's addictive. You know? She's very insistent and present. She is volatile and wonderful and everywhere."

"Everywhere."

A succinct nod. "Everywhere. Once that connection is made."

"Why wasn't she around you? When I was young?"

"I had to leave her behind. I had to move on to better things. Other things."

"Like?"

"You and your mother, of course. Family. My own. I had to choose. You or her. And then I had to choose to protect you from *her."*

"But she's here."

"You found her."

"Why didn't you get rid of it?"

"The book?"

"Yeah."

"You can't. Once it's yours, it's yours."

He turned to look at the book and realized he didn't know where it was.

That made him think that it was lurking. Lingering somewhere, watching and waiting for him. But not the book.

Her.

He turned to ask his father one of a million questions at war in his mind and he saw the horns first. A rack of them. Ten points? Twelve? Twenty?

How could a human head hold them up?

It's not a human head, though, is it?

She was in profile.

Before his eyes she flickered like a glitching video. His father—her horned head—his dad—her visage—his dad…

"If you feed her you can see me again. But choose wisely," his dad said.

Then Andrew's eyes flared wide and he looked alarmed.

Was he realizing that even dead he could catch her ire?

She fully showed up then. Pale skin, wild eyes, fierce hair. A tangle of horns and knots and a dry sound that he realized was her horns scraping along the exposed beam ceiling overhead and her toenails—talons—claws? —scraping the cement floor of the workroom.

She held out a long pole with a knife fashioned onto the tip. It looked like a diving knife. And he knew if he studied it well it would bear the marks STAINLESS STEEL, #515, Japan.

One of his father's knives.

He took it.

CHAPTER 19

WHEN HE WOKE it was raining and he was crying. He held the crudely fashioned spear, startled and terrified that it existed.

Had he made it in his sleep? Some sort of sleepwalking incident?

Had his father been here? Her?

Somehow, it had come into existence, and he felt sick to his stomach because he knew exactly what it was for.

Steve.

The question was, did they expect him to go today or tomorrow?

"What are you doing? What the fuck are you doing? He's a person. Random scraps of flesh and fingertips and teeth are bad enough. But to..." He shook his head and ran a hand through his hair. The hand was shaking very badly.

Ben realized then that the lights were back on. He went and blew out the candles one at a time.

"Dad, Jesus fucking Christ, Dad. If that was you—if you were there, I mean, here—help me. You have to be able to. Aren't you supposed to be all magical and shit after you die? Somehow?"

He knew that wasn't true, though. Any more than God was real. It was all a delusion that people shared to feel safer. To feel like they didn't have to be responsible in their own lives. If they failed, God was testing them. If they succeeded, it was thanks to him.

Why did they beg for his help when their children went missing or got sick but praise him when some small success happened in life?

Give all the glory to God, he'd heard people say.

Give all the gory to god.

In his mind's eye flashed her crown of horns.

Chills raced through him and he realized he was sweating.

He kept the spear in his hand because he didn't know what else to do. He turned off the lights, pulled the workroom door shut, and went up the steps slowly.

He was in the kitchen eating a peanut butter and pickle sandwich when someone knocked on the door.

Christ. Who was it now? This many people hadn't knocked for him in years, and now suddenly, in the last few days, he was Mister Popularity.

He went to the door, wiping his hands on the seat of his jeans.

Alice Day. Trying very hard to peek through the peephole.

It made him laugh.

He pulled the door open. "Hey. I was going to text you."

She sniffed. "You smell like peanut butter."

"Good nose."

"I'm starving."

He liked that she wasn't shy about asking for stuff. She didn't do the annoying cryptic never asks for what she wants thing so many girls did.

"Want a sandwich?"

"Yes, I do. Whatever you had."

"Peanut butter and pickle."

She looked intrigued. "Ooh, exotic. I'm in."

He made her a sandwich as she tried to woo Solace out from under the butcher block.

She had a mouthful of sandwich and a cold bottle of water in her hand when she said, "Did he have it?"

"Yep. He did. It's on the coffee table."

"You. Are. The. Best." She popped the last bite into her mouth and wolfed it down. Then she grabbed his shoulders, tugged him forward and kissed him.

On the mouth.

Hard.

With tongue.

Electricity shot through his body and he thought he might burst into flames.

He almost stiff-armed her. Remembering the hungry woman who lived in his book, his head, his home.

But he'd given her a tooth and Alice was off-limits. So was Solace.

His mind flitted to Steve in a dark hole in the ground. He thought of his father. The stick with a knife tip. The feel of that tooth in his hand. And a fingertip in his pocket.

He hadn't realized he was hard until she stepped toward him and closed the gap between them. Instead of stiff-arming her, he pulled her against him.

He fell into the kiss. Sank into it. Grateful he'd gotten all the weird clunky kiss practice out of the way last year with Maryellen Donovan.

She felt it. And in his mind, he froze like a deer in headlights.

But she didn't back up and she didn't stop kissing him.

His fingers curled around the tops of her arms. Her skin soft and warm against his.

She moved against him. Deliberately. And his brain turned nearly feral.

He had a very distinct image in his mind of himself pushing her thighs apart, sliding between them, moving into her.

He could see it all perfectly.

Vividly.

Like a picture in a book—

He stepped back, sucking in a gasp.

"You okay?" she cocked her head. Her nipples were hard inside her made-to-look-vintage Muppets tee.

Ben had to swallow a moan.

"Fine. Fine. I just—I have somewhere I have to go, and I just remembered."

Her eyes looked glazed. Drunken.

She seemed to come around. She looked at her surroundings like she'd just woken from a dream.

But then she smiled and said, "Okay. Sorry."

"No sorry needed. I'm just a fucking moron, I forgot."

They walked into the living room and she picked up the manual.

"Not a fucking moron. My fucking hero!" She looked down then up at him with those brown velvet eyes. "You'll come?" She waved the book, so he knew what she meant, but his brain still tripped over the choice of word.

"I will."

Then she was gone. Looking lean, beautiful, and cool in the blistering sunlight of the afternoon.

Ben shut and locked the door. Then he walked up to his room, pulled his shorts down, and shut his eyes, picturing her. Perfect and smiling.

"You'll come?" she'd asked.

Ben made sure he did just that.

CHAPTER 20

HE HAD to walk the whole way to Steve's. The back way. It was hard enough to walk with a crudely fashioned spear. He couldn't imagine trying to ride a bike.

He didn't know what he was supposed to do. Or why he was doing it. He only knew that somehow, this was the tradeoff for Alice.

He had looked inside the book before he'd left the house. For the first time ever, he's found it in the middle of its dark task. Half the tooth was gone. Half the root. All the dried blood. A previously invisible cavity now showed, and he wondered if Steve even knew he had a cavity in that tooth.

If anyone stopped him, he had his boy-scout-camping-trip-survival-training-my-dad-was-a-prepper speech worked out.

But he went along the dusty back streets that were nearly glorified alleys. He passed the backs of houses nicer than his and some way worse.

He pushed the knife tip through the dirt, swatted a tree. He wondered how hard he'd have to stab with this to actually puncture anything.

The diving knife was either deliberately on the blunt side, dulled by time, or had never been sharp to begin with.

He poked a tree to get a feel and felt the resistance.

That was a tree, though.

Finally, he found a tree with crab apples on it. Small hard, misshapen fruit that seemed to glower in the sun.

He stood still and stabbed at one of them.

It wasn't very easy since it was on the branch and the whole thing swayed when he came in contact with the fruit.

The small apple bobbed away from the seeking silver tip when he tried a second time.

"God damn it," he said through gritted teeth.

He tried once more, aiming for a bigger one, wanting to feel the puncture-pop of the skin and flesh being pierced.

Instead, he stumbled because he missed the apple and the momentum carried him forward, the spear jabbing harmlessly between branches.

"Fuck! Fuck fuck fuck!"

He froze, a deer stood there. A fawn. Ear twitching. Eyes wide. She was frozen with fear and slightly boxed in between tall skinny trees set close together.

But then Ben felt a calmness flowed over him. A kismet moment.

He steadied his breath and his mind. And then he rushed the three steps between them, wielding the spear, and he felt it drive into the side of the small Disney movie creature.

She let out a bleat. A high-toned one. She quivered and kicked, and he put his weight behind it, then. Leaning into the movement.

He felt the knife push between ribs. Part meat. Sever things that shouldn't be severed if a creature was to remain living.

He felt an elation very akin to a breathtaking orgasm. And he stood there looking at her. Gloriously beautiful in her death throes.

Pulling out the spear, he shoved his fingers into the wound. Pushed and tugged and yanked until he felt his fingers close around something small and very warm. He pulled it out. Almost positive it was the heart.

Whatever it was. It had been alive. And the book didn't seem to be finicky.

His mood had improved. His question answered. He'd have to stab very hard with the spear. But could he do it?

He got back on the road, smeared with blood, the heart wrapped in some leaves and stuck in his cargo shorts pocket.

When he saw the trap door coming into sight. His dick got hard again.

He should feel shame. He should feel guilt.

The scary part was Ben felt as if he'd elevated past those feelings. Transcended.

He could hear Steve screaming before he opened the trap door.

He pushed the rocks to the side, propped the spear against the tree, and pulled up the latch.

Steve's head tipped back, pale white and dirty, streaked with blood in the sudden splash of sunlight.

Naked relief, so pure it was palpable, washed over the boy's face.

"You're back." His laugh was a rasp. "You came back. You're just fucking with me. It went too far, man. You really hurt me, Ben. But it's fine. It's fine. Help me out so I can get my tooth looked at."

Ben stared down at him. Even from above, he could see the fluttering at the boy's throat. His heart was beating at a runaway pace.

Steve was afraid. He could tell by the way his words tumbled over each other.

"I have your tooth," Ben said.

"I know. I meant, the spot where it was."

"Stand still," Ben said.

He tried to see in the gloom all around the bunker. His eyes strained. And then she was there. In the dark behind Steve.

Poor Steve.

Poor, poor Steve.

When Ben blinked, she was closer.

Another blink.

Closer still.

She lurked there. As if to wrap her horrible arms around the boy from behind.

"Stand still," Ben said again.

CHAPTER 21

THE NOISE WAS GRISTLY. Meaty.

The scream that came out of Steve was otherworldly. It hurt Ben's ears and made the hair on his nape stand up despite the pounding heat of the day.

There was a thrill of power knowing that no one could hear them. That no one was even looking yet.

"Why?"

"I need it," Ben said. "Throw it up."

"No!"

"Throw it up or I'll do it again."

He could see her in there behind the boy. Watching. She wanted what he had but couldn't get it herself. She needed Ben. He needed her. He wasn't sure why. But he did.

Steve was down there sobbing. Holding his head. Blood streaming through his fingers.

"Why are you doing this?"

"Just throw it up."

"You have to let me out."

"Not yet. Soon," Ben lied.

"Why are you doing this?" Steve screamed it at the top of his lungs. Ben felt the vibration of it. Yet, he felt no fear of being discovered.

The bunker was too far off. And she was too wise to let them be heard.

Because I can.

"Throw it up and I'll throw you a water."

"I have water!"

"Do you?"

Steve stopped and hung his head.

Ben had seen snacks strewn around down there when he'd briefly entered. But nothing to drink. Certainly, no fridge. No cooler. But still…

The ear lofted into the air. Ben almost missed it. At the last minute, he stuck his hand out and plucked the flesh seashell from the air.

He put it in the pocket of his cargo shorts. The other pocket held the heart that seeped wetness against his leg.

He pulled out the water bottle from his back pocket and dropped it straight down.

Steve tried to catch it but missed. It bounced and rolled into the shadows.

Ben caught the glimmer of her silvery eyes looking out from the black edges of the bunker.

He was suddenly very tired.

"I'll be back."

"Ben. Why? Why are you doing th—"

Ben slammed the door and found the heavy rocks. He stacked them on top, kicked leaves and limbs over the door, making sure it was hidden well.

He was only about a hundred yards away from the bunker when he heard someone coming.

He dropped the spear into the brush and moved a few feet away from it.

A guy walking his dog. The man looked up, saw Ben. The dog strained on the leash, angling toward him.

The man took a good look at Ben. Blood streaming down his leg where the heart was leaking in his pocket. Some smeared on his shirt, his hands.

The guy stopped short.

After a long moment—too long for Ben's comfort—he asked, "You okay?"

Ben put on his best grin. It felt like a death rictus stretched across his face. And yet, he kept it plastered there.

"Fine. Took a tumble a ways back on my hike. I think I hit every rock and branch on the way down."

The guy winced sympathetically. "Ouch."

Again, his little black and white dog strained against the leash and whined. The man took a step toward Ben as if to follow the dog's lead.

It all flashed through his mind then. The heart in his pocket, the ear in the other, the deer blood and human blood on him. The spear there in the grass.

"Please," he said, putting his hands out. "Don't let her come near me. I'm very allergic."

That stopped him instantly. "Oh. Sorry. You sure you're okay? Do you need me to go get someone? Or call someone?"

Ben put the smile back on his aching face. "Nope. I'm good. I'm headed home now. A good hot shower and some Tylenol and I should be okay."

The man gave him one more less than convinced once over and then tugged the leash. The dog went insane, but after a moment, he convinced her to come along and leave the bloody teenager alone.

When they were finally out of sight, Ben finally exhaled.

He found his spear, doubled back to the bunker, and hid the spear in the bushes and weeds to the left of the door. Best to leave it behind. He'd be much less conspicuous walking home bloody minus a makeshift weapon.

Eyes burning, he slogged home. His steps heavy.

It only occurred to him when he was about a block away that the ear would be a stretch, fitting it into the book. But the heart—as small as it might be—there was no way in hell it would fit.

CHAPTER 22

SHE HAD THOUGHT OF THAT, apparently. When he went to find the book, in the basement—had he left it in the basement?—He found the bowl.

Not an average bowl. A large bowl with a shallow but wide depression, fashioned of two interlocking sets of antlers. The tips worked together to form the recess for his offerings. The severed ends where the antlers would have attached to the animal stuck up, beckoning to the ceiling.

He stood there looking at it, knowing everything would change. Knowing there was no turning back after this. This meant the woman was either real and had supplied this vessel or she was not real but could manipulate reality. Non-corporeal but able to manipulate the corporeal world.

Ben didn't know which was more terrifying.

His phone started to vibrate. His mother.

He looked at the picture of her that illuminated his screen. It was a picture from when his dad was still alive. Her face looked happy. She looked connected. When he looked into her eyes, he saw something.

His throat grew tight, and he double clicked the side button to reject the call.

He sat in the gold wingback and waited for the phone to buzz again signifying a voicemail.

After a moment it did.

He put it on speakerphone.

"Ben? Benny? You didn't answer again…"

There was a long pause where he felt his blood heat up and his stomach bottom out. He wanted to punch her. Tear at her. Make her bleed. Put pieces of her into the book and—

"I wanted to let you know…" Sniffle sniffle sniffle. He rolled his eyes. "…I'll be home soon. I broke up with Patrick."

Her pause was hopeful this time as if he'd answer the phone now that she'd admitted this bit of news.

"If he shows up. Well, if he shows up there, you tell him I'm not back yet and I don't want to see him when I do get back. He was a bad person to have around. I know that now. It wasn't good for you. For me…or us. I'm sorry. I'll be back soon. I promise."

"Don't bother," he said to the empty room. "I'm learning I don't need you."

He was bold when he opened the book this time. He flipped it open cavalierly and saw the tooth was gone and she stood facing him. Smiling. Looking like a terrible benefactor. A dark protector.

"I brought you something," he said. "But you knew that already."

A decision had to be made. Did she get the heart? Did she get the ear?

"Appetizers first," he sing-songed. The sound of his own voice, a lunatic melody, made his skin prickle.

Ben moved toward it, heart in hand. Part of him waiting for the antlers to clamp toward one another—much like Audrey II in Little Shop of Horrors—and slurp him inside.

But he didn't think it wanted him. It wanted his offerings.

At least for the moment.

The heart was slippery in his hand as he went to put it in. Maybe it was nerves and he didn't want to get too close. The image of those antlers clamping shut on him, trapping him, digging into his flesh wouldn't leave his mind.

The heart slid out of his hand at the last moment and dropped into the deepest part of the bowl.

He stared at it, as if it would get sucked down into some great vortex.

Instead, it sat there, dark and bloody. Still.

He sat down in the old reading chair and ran a hand through his hair. It was dirty and sweaty and stuck up in clumps.

He needed a haircut. His mother usually cut it.

"I don't know what you want. I hope that works," he said, tired.

His eyes drooped again. The second time today.

Was it the stress or the heat? Was it the woman in the book?

He shut his eyes and tried to relax, but he could feel the ear burning against his thigh. The dried blood making his pants stiff.

"Dad, I don't know what I'm doing."

Funny how his sole parent was only viable in dreams. Funny how the only thing watching over him in the real world was some sort of book demon.

He snorted.

His father had always told him that deep down, no one really knew what they were doing. We are all just winging it.

"But my winging it is hurting people. At least I haven't killed anyone." He said it as a joke. He said it to make himself feel better. But an unspoken *yet* seemed to quiver and echo in the silence around him.

The boiler kicked on and he jumped.

Their basement was hotter than the average basement. The big rumbling machine always kept it tepid. Easy to fall asleep in the heat when it was actively running.

Rest...

That wasn't him. It wasn't the ghost of his dad. It was her voice. Something between a quivering trill and a hiss.

There was a sinister kind of comfort in it.

He shut his eyes all the way—they burned like he had a fever—and went still.

He heard his father humming from the workroom. He heard him puttering around. Organizing, cleaning up, touching screws and nails and tape and childhood treasures.

It was a soothing sound. The sound of home.

He dreams. And in his dream, he goes to the antler bowl and peers inside.

It's empty. And hungry. He places the ear inside. Gently this time. No fear. A reverence.

His father is proud.

CHAPTER 23

"Where is she then?"

Pain coursed through Ben's forehead just above his left eye. He sat up and then instantly sat back after getting a face full of reeking alcohol breath.

Patrick. His breath spoke of many rounds and a long time in the dark womb of a bar.

"What? Who?"

His poor brain was struggling to catch up to what was happening.

Behind the man, hulking over him, he saw the thorny extensions of the antler bowl. He saw a flash of black, a swaying sea of silvery hair, the smell of swamp and loam and sudden thunderstorms.

The hair on his forearms stood at attention. His ears rang.

"Your fucking mother! Where is she?" Patrick boomed.

He was very far gone. But not the far gone that wound down into singing old songs, telling ancient stories, and laughing wetly.

No. He was far gone into the realm of screaming his wants while spittle flew from his lips.

"She's not here," Ben said.

His eyes studied the shadows in the corners of the basement. He could see in the small rectangle of the window that it was dark out. So, well past nine at night.

The thick smoky dream of getting up to drop the ear into the antler bowl came to him.

Had he? Had he done that? Or dreamt it?

He was yanked out of his reverie when Patrick grabbed the collar of his tee and shook him vigorously. Ben's head snapped forward and then back. It rapped the headrest of the ancient chair. So old the padding had long since flattened.

He saw stars.

"Where is that cunt? She had to have called you. Telling me we're over. Telling me to get lost. I'll cut her tits off—"

"Go ahead!" Ben screamed back. His spit speckled Patrick's mottled face dark with more than two days' worth of beard. "I don't fucking care. And get the fuck off me."

He pushed the other man hard. Patrick stumbled back, hit a book-shelf, and almost—*alllllllmost*—went ass first into that antler bowl.

So close.

His brown eyes flared with anger as he righted himself. Tugging his collar down like a well-dressed man who'd been mussed on his way to a meeting as opposed to a fucking drunk who'd gotten manhandled.

"You little shit." He lunged for Ben who dodged easily.

Patrick crashed into the wall, knocked a dartboard off its nail, and bounced. He went down on his ass on the rag rug.

"You fuck!"

Ben didn't think about it. He kicked him. In the head. Hard. So hard his foot seized up in a Charley horse. So, he slammed it down on the ground and kicked the man with the other foot.

"You piece of shit. You cocksucker. You asshole!" All the rage in him came bubbling up, toxic and copious.

Every time the man had muttered, *twat, pussy, mama's boy*, or the like flashed back to him.

He kicked him again.

Patrick groaned as his jaw snapped shut and his teeth clacked loud like a twig snapping. He must have bitten his tongue because blood ran down his chin and his eyes rolled crazily.

Ben felt joy. Sheer and sudden joy. Victory. Power.

So many months of this guy. So much to deal with after having to process the death of his father. He'd lost one parent. And then swiftly lost the remaining one—to this stupid fuck. This drunk.

He kicked him again. And again. And again. Gore flew but Ben kept going.

He kicked him until the air whistled in and out of Patrick's muti-lated nose and the shattered remains of his teeth. A single spectacular blood bubble swelled, growing like an engorged tick. Ben kicked him again, watching the bubble burst with a vibrant spray. Patrick's groaning finally turned to wet gagging. But Ben kept going. He kicked him until shards of teeth got embedded in the soft meat of the arch of his foot and he was bleeding too.

He kicked him until he heard sobbing and realized it was his own.

He kicked him until that hand snaked out from the shadowy corner of the room and curled beckoning fingers toward the antler bowl.

Ben stopped and he pushed his hands under Patrick's limp body.

He was still alive. Still moving. But just barely.

Ben dragged him up by the collar of his shirt until they were face to pulpy, dripping face. The realization that he had done that hit home. His hands had busted that skin, shattered those teeth, turned flesh and blood into human soup. He stared at the man as he bully-walked him backward. A drunken stumbling dance.

Then he pushed him with all his might.

Patrick landed ass first in the bowl. The momentum of his body carrying him back until the squelching crunch-pop of the seeking tips of the severed antlers punctured him. They appeared through his skin like pussy willows in the spring. Small buds breaching the fabric of his shirt. Blood oozed.

Patrick gave him one last bewildered stare through eyes that could barely open. One ruined socket leaked clear fluid in place of actual tears. Then Patrick exhaled slowly.

And for the last time.

In his bed, hair still wet from a shower, Ben stared at the shifting miasma of shadows. Pixilated like a movie, they undulated. A trick of the eye no doubt. He wondered if she was in those shadows. If she was done eating. If she still wanted more.

And what else would she expect of him?

He thought he heard something. Ears straining to hear it again but picking up nothing but the ringing of silence.

Was she in the shadows?

He hoped so.

CHAPTER 24

"You know you shouldn't have taken in that stray."

Cold water ran down Ben's spine.

"Why not?"

"Too tempting." His father was making eggs and toast and bacon. His Sunday morning ritual. "She's coming into it all now. Gaining strength."

His father chuckled. He set the eggs in front of Ben and said, "Speaking of strength. You need to eat, too. You're too skinny. And you skipped dinner."

He had skipped dinner, he realized. Too tired after dealing with Patrick.

"She can't spare Solace?"

"Every family is built on love and sacrifice," his father said.

A heaviness settled over Ben. But he shoveled the food in because he realized as soon as he put a bite in his mouth, just how ravenous he was. Was this how she felt? Was she this hungry?

"I know but—"

"No buts," his father said. Shaking his head, the way he did when he'd entertain no argument. "You like seeing me?"

"Yes."

"You want a family?"

"Yes."

"A real one. One that sticks around and looks after you?"

"Of course."

"Then a little sacrifice here and there is needed."

Ben wanted to say a little about the sacrifices he'd made, but he didn't *want to upset the balance. Family was important. Something few knew until they lost it.*

"It will be okay. We'll get you a new pet. Later. When things calm down."

When things calm down...

He went on eating.

"What about Mom?" *he finally asked.*

His father stopped. "What about her?"

"When she comes back? What will happen?"

His father blew out a breath. The sound he made when he was weary with thought. "Do you think she even deserves to be your mother anymore?"

"Not really." *It was the truth. Grief had been hard. Harder with having to help her put herself back together every day.*

She'd lost her husband, yes. But he'd lost his father. A fact she seemed to never fully comprehend.

Her inability to understand that hurt almost as much as the loss of his dad.

"Hey, don't sweat it. I'm here now."

"I know."

"We'll be fine. Family is what you make of it. If life gives you a shitty family—make your own."

Somewhere downstairs the cat screamed. Ben sat up. Heart pounding. He waited, listening.

After a while, he laid back down. Guilt made it hard to fall back asleep.

He hoped he didn't dream.

He didn't bother looking for Solace. He knew her fate and half wished he'd never brought her into the house. But he hadn't known and maybe it had to be that way.

Some stuff needed to happen for others to happen. Or something like that.

He ate a handful of Peanut M&Ms and had a bottle of iced tea. Standing over the air conditioning vent, he let it blow up the leg of his shorts.

It was hot outside. It could be felt even inside the house.

He stared blankly at the water and food bowl on the mat. He put them in the dishwasher and then threw out the litter pan. The remaining cat food went in the trash.

He did all of this to avoid going into the basement and looking at the offering bowl. What would he find? Nothing? Bones? A dead man staring accusingly up at him.

Finally, he flipped on the lights and went down.

The dehumidifier clicked on, making him jump.

When he entered the reading area, he saw the antler bowl. Pure, pristine, and unstained. Inside were a pile of clothes, a watch, a wallet, a St. Christopher's medal, and a pack of cigarettes with a lighter.

There was a rattling of metal when he gathered up the bundle. He looked into the bowl to see what had fallen. A handful of what looked like pewter or silver rocks and a long thin pin made of metal.

He picked them up and shook them. Aware of the crawling sensation that was the fear of those antlers snapping shut around his reaching hand and holding him inside.

Ben started laughing. Once he started, he couldn't stop.

Fillings. He was holding a handful of fillings. And a single surgical pin.

What was the injury Patrick had claimed to have? Usually, when physical labor was required. Some football injury for which he'd had surgery.

"Sensitive stomach?" Ben said, by way of making a joke. "Can't she digest this?"

He took the clothes out to the backyard and built a small fire in the fire pit. They used to sit around it on fall nights when things were better. When things were *good*.

His mother with a glass of wine, his father with a beer, him with a hot chocolate or a warm cider. They'd let him feed leaves into the flames. Just one at a time. You weren't supposed to burn leaves, his father always reminded him. But who was going to take issue with one at a time?

Then he'd wink.

Now he let it get nice and high. Let the flames lick the edges of the pit and then shoot above.

He fed the tee in. Sweaty, mangled in spots. The fire lapped at it. Consumed it. Turned it into ash. Next were the jeans. The socks. The shoes he tossed in the old shed for later. Burning them seemed like a bad idea. Then the contents of the wallet. One by one until the air reeked of burning plastic and charred leather.

He took the metal bits out to the back of the yard and tossed them one by one into the thick, overgrown brush and weeds. Good luck finding those.

Not that he thought anyone would come looking for Patrick. No one would care.

The grate came down with a clack and he watched the flames tease along the diamond-shaped openings seeking oxygen and freedom.

"You can't be cold," came a voice.

Ben jumped a mile, hand to his heart. He turned to the gate to see Alice. Alice Day with her shock of chaotic hair and her big smile.

The sensation of falling swept over him for a moment and he widened his stance to steady himself.

"Nope. Just burning some stuff. Pass the time." He tried on a shrug and it fit. He walked toward her, not as tense.

He was in control. This was fine.

"You know, I kissed you."

"I know."

"I like you."

"I like you, too." He was shocked he'd had the nerve to say it. Once upon a time, he wouldn't have dared admit it. But a lot had changed over the last few days.

"I thought you'd invite me to stay," she said.

There was no way he was reading this right. No way she was hinting toward more. She was a little over a year older than him and he had no idea if she was a virgin. He didn't care one way or another. He liked Alice.

A lot.

But the thought of her being in his house with (the mother) the woman in the book. No. Alice was one thing he wouldn't give her.

"Sorry. I think my mom's boyfriend might be stopping by. We don't get along. They broke up…" He let it peter off and shrugged. "It's a whole thing."

"Ah, a thing. Well…" She glanced past him. "Your fire's almost out."

"And?"

"We could go for a walk."

"Let's go."

CHAPTER 25

EVERYTHING WAS SO lush and green. They'd gone back the way he and Mikey had. He thought about taking her to the shack or the tunnels. Just to show her something cool.

Instead, he took her hand when she offered it, and they took off down a foreign trail.

"The party is in a week," she said.

"I'll be there." And he would. Regardless of what happened. He wanted to go.

"Why have you never told me you liked me?" She kept her gaze forward and a small smile played across her mouth.

He wanted to stop, turn her, kiss that mouth. Kiss her and then kiss her some more.

The urge was almost unbearable, but he also didn't trust himself the way he once had. Best not to tempt the darkness in him.

He was a killer now. He had lost a part of himself. But found another part.

"I was shyer then."

"Then?" She laughed. "It was a few weeks ago."

He laughed, squeezed her hand. "I know."

They crested a hill. She wasn't even breathing hard. Or sweating. He was doing both.

"And now?"

They stopped and stared at the sight before them.

"Now, things are different," he said.

"Wow," she said.

"Right? Weird."

There was a pond. Shallow, no doubt. Because in the very center sat a dining room chair. The shore to the pond was overgrown with green. Wild vines, flowers, long grasses, and reeds. The water was clear. Clearer than any water he'd ever seen.

"That's insane," she said, already walking toward it.

Sunlight shone down on the water and the chair like a spotlight. A clearing that was clear for no apparent reason.

She pulled off her sneakers, her shorts, and her tank before he could even think. She walked across the lush grass and dipped a toe in the water.

"Cool, not cold," she said.

His gaze settled on her collarbone. The lovely hollows. The small swell of breasts inside the black sports bra. The flat of her belly. The very shine of her dark skin in the dappled sunlight. His gaze lingered at the spot just above her waistband. Her sex was accented by her white cotton panties.

His head buzzed, his cock strained.

He was way too tired to test his restraint. Way too out of sorts to fight his wants.

"Come on in," she said, turning away from him.

She walked toward the chair. Why was it there? Was it simply a matter of someone playing a joke? Was it all dry until a certain time of year?

Too many questions.

No answers.

Why were there tunnels? Why that shack with someone clearly living in it out in the middle of the woods? Why was there a hungry creature in his house with a maternal instinct?

Why was he now a predator?

He shucked his sneaker and his shorts. His boxer briefs did absolutely zero to hide his hard-on.

He was sixteen, headed towards seventeen. Brushing his hair gave him a hard-on. Whereas once he'd have been mortified and embarrassed, now he was nonchalant.

She saw it and smiled shyly. But she didn't turn away.

She bent and cupped the water in her hands. Stared into it. "It's so clear," she said, dumping it on her chest. Then she sighed contently. "That feels so good. It's ridiculously hot."

This somehow smacked of the woman, but did her power over him extend outside of the house? Influence him or other things?

That was crazy.

But then he thought of Steve, still in a hole in the ground. His tooth. His fear. The urge to do all that. To hunt and gather and provide for his family and—

She walked toward him and he cut off his own train of thought.

The woman was in his head. That was it. And that was okay. Maternal. Protector. Present.

Alice wanted him to touch her. He could see it. Smell it. Sense it.

And it was all meant to be and totally okay.

He reached for her and she smiled. He pulled her close and she came. He wrapped his arms around her and she responded. The kiss was fire. A willing clash of urgent needs.

She pushed him back suddenly and he thought he'd overstepped. Ready to back off, he only caught on when she pushed him again. Playfully. Toward the strange chair that stood in the center of the pond.

He'd never done this before. Never been with a girl. But his body seemed to know its role and its needs. He followed the rhythm of instinct.

He walked backward, keeping his hand on her hips. They'd been flirting all year. But he'd been too shy, too unsure. And now, he wanted what was right in front of him

She gave him another little push and his ass hit the seat. His boxer briefs left no need for imagination on how he felt about the situation.

She reached into her bra and pulled out a purple foil package.

She held it, sat on his lap. He felt the heat of her on his crotch and his heart skipped a beat.

Here in the spotlight of blazing sun, it felt so safe. So far away from a world full of teeth and severed fingertips, dead drunken men, and missing kittens.

But it felt contrived too. He was smart enough to feel that.

"Have you been with anyone before?"

"No. Does it matter?"

"Nope." She kissed him.

"Have you?" he asked, already suspecting the answer.

"Yes," she said. "Does it matter?"

"Nope."

He gripped her hips tightly and willed her to lean in. She did. She leaned in and he kissed her. Then she was fingers, smooth and cool, on his hard skin. The kiss of latex. The shooting star sensation of her handling him, positioning him, taking him in.

In the warm sun, with the streamers of weeping willows encircling them, he lost his virginity. On a weird old wooden chair, feet wet in the weirdest pond he'd ever seen.

He moved up under her and none of it lasted very long, but the ending was sweet and sudden.

He was concerned about her and she smiled, brushing it off. But he didn't let her. So she showed him what to do, how to make it sweet for her too, and he did.

They sat there then in the silence; the woods seemed to have grown hushed around them. Listening. Not breathing.

"I have to get home," she said softly. Lips murmuring against his neck.

He felt a sinking sadness.

"I'll walk you."

They walked to her house hand in hand. He tried to stay right there in the moment. Not thinking about home or what might come when he got there.

She kissed him at the door. "You'll come to my party."

"Of course." He grinned. "I've told you a million times."

"I'll see you soon?" She seemed uncertain. Nervous now.

"Yes. Very soon."

She didn't seem to believe him, and he hoped he was telling her the truth.

He walked home slowly. Not in much of a hurry for the glow of the day to be gone.

CHAPTER 26

THE WORDS SWAM UP.

He'd gone right to the book as if hearing it sing to him.

He'd expected maybe a demand for more. Or something stuck in the book. But instead, she faced him now on the page. Despite being fully facing him, she was still draped in shadows. The thorns of her horns glistened like they were bloody.

His eyes focused on the word MOTHER.

Then an assault: MOTHERMOTHERMOTHERMOTH-ERMOTHER

Whether it meant she was claiming him as her own or she was talking about his actual mother, he had no idea. And he was too freaked out to ask.

Then the word FAMILY.

Followed by FATHER.

Then MOTHERPROTECTORMOTHERMOTHER

Then finally, as expected: MORE

MOREMOREMOREMOREMORE

"Yes, more. I know. I'll get you more. For now, I'm tired. So tired."

He shut the book. After a moment, he put the hurricane lamp on top. An ashtray. And a stack of other books.

He laid down on the sofa and thought about his time with Alice. How it had come out of the blue. How it had been a bright and shining spot in the middle of all this confusion.

He realized he had forgotten all about Steve. He wondered if he was there in the dark sipping water and waiting. Had he managed to get out?

No. If he had, they'd have come for Ben by now.

He waited, expecting to feel guilt. Expecting to feel remorse and fear. To feel sick over it.

He did not.

He felt tired. And he felt safe.

He fell asleep.

※

The knock woke him. The cable box told him it was 10:07. It was dark.

He flipped on the lamp on the end table and tried to get his bearings. He'd crashed hard. No dreams. Just deep and unremarkable sleep.

The knock came again.

"Coming!"

He looked out to see Steve's sister standing there.

His heart pounded, but he didn't hesitate to unlock and open the door.

"Hey, there—um…"

"Amanda," she said.

"Right. Amanda. Hey, what's up?"

She sighed. "Have you seen Steve?"

He shook his head. "Not since the other day at your place. Why?"

She looked worried. No longer bored and annoyed with her younger brother's friend. She looked pale and haunted and tired.

"He hasn't come home since that day. He left with you and then never came back. Where did you go?"

"We went for a walk in the woods," he said. "I had to leave. I offered to walk him home, but he said he was fine and to just go on. So, I went." The lies rolled off his tongue easily. More easily than a truth ever had with a stranger.

He'd always been awkward and quiet to a degree. Unless he was with people he knew and felt comfortable around.

Amanda would have muted him as easily as his remote silenced his TV.

"Damn." She sighed. "I told my parents I'd check with you. I had to figure out who you were, to be honest, but once I did I promised and…we're just worried. Really. And if you hear from him can you let us know or bring him home or tell him to call or something."

"Is there any reason he'd leave?" Ben asked, curious if there was. It would make a good excuse.

"Him and my dad have been having it out. We thought he was pouting. Or just trying to scare my parents. But at this point, it doesn't matter why, we want him to come home."

Ben nodded, putting on his best concerned and empathetic face. "I'll make sure to let you know if I hear from him. Or if he calls."

"Thanks," she said. "I appreciate it."

Then she was gone in the dark.

He waited. Expecting a remnant of his old self, his old conscience, to rise up and make him head out in the night to let Steve out of the hole. Make up an excuse. Apologize for the terrible prank.

Instead, he shuffled up to bed, leaving the TV on for noise. He'd deal with Steve in the morning.

CHAPTER 27

HE RODE his bike to the bunker. It was 89 degrees at seven a.m. Horrible.

Ben had woken early. He found himself starving. His phone was dead so he plugged it in to charge. It had died sometime while he was asleep on the sofa and spent the night on the living room end table.

It burbled missed notifications and texts at him, but he was too busy making a whole roll of breakfast sausage found in the back of the freezer and eating it as fast as it cooked.

He regarded the nearly empty freezer and found a frozen waffle which he promptly nuked, smeared with butter and jelly, and ate folded in half like a limp taco.

He could practically hear his father laughing in his head.

The house had an air of occupancy now. Like it was just more than him here. Which was odd, because the only other living thing that had occupied it with him had (been consumed) disappeared. But the house had that sunshiny full of life feel.

He went the roundabout way so as not to pass Steve's house then walked slowly down the dirt path toward the bunker. His shoes kicking up dust. It hadn't rained in days and the storms they'd had a few days back had been sudden and violent and fleeting. The water running off faster than the ground could absorb it.

The heat was high, the humidity higher, and the cicadas screamed their mating calls, desperately lonely.

He found the spear where he'd hidden it and dropped it at his feet near the metal hatch door. It only took a few minutes to clear the brush and move the big rocks.

He listened before opening the door and heard what sounded like a weak voice, but he wasn't sure if that was real or his imagination.

When he flipped the door up, he waited. Silence for a moment.

Had Steve simply died? That would almost be a relief. Because then he wouldn't have to make any kind of decision.

He put his backpack down at his feet and unzipped it.

Then it came. "Hello? Is someone there?"

"It's me," Ben called down, unsure of what else to say.

Steve didn't hurry to greet him. Ben couldn't blame him.

"Are you going to let me out now?"

"Maybe." Ben felt no guilt lying. He found that somehow impressive.

"Why are you doing this?"

"It's a long story."

"I have time." Steve laughed. It was a high untethered laugh that spoke of a fracturing psyche.

"Come into the light."

"I don't want to."

"I won't hurt you," Ben said.

Another laugh.

Finally, Steve dragged himself into the light.

Ben was surprised by how much weight he'd lost being down there for just a few days.

"I'm really thirsty."

"You drank all your water?"

"Yeah." Steve sighed. It was the sound of a tired old man.

"I didn't bring any with me. I will next time. I brought you something else, though."

"Food?"

"No," Ben said. He dug around in the backpack.

"You could just let me up. I won't tell anyone it was you. or what happened. I just…" There was a sniffle, but Steve's face remained dry. He was probably too dehydrated to cry. "I just want to go home. To my family. To my bed."

"Soon," Ben lied.

He pulled the book out and opened it. There she was. The (mother) woman. Staring at him. Suspended in shadows but fully visible. Horns and hungry eyes and wild raucous hair.

"I brought you something to read," he said.

He had no idea if this would work, but bringing the book to the bunker seemed way easier than trying to bring Steve to the sacrificial bowl.

So he tossed it down.

Steve caught it, reflexively. "I don't have much light, Ben. And I'm too tired to read."

"It's fine. It'll be fine."

Then he slammed the door and put the rocks back. He'd come back later for the book.

And to see what had happened.

⚜

He took a walk. It was too hot to walk but he needed to clear his head. Or fill it. One or the other.

He walked down to the 7-11 on the corner and bought himself a Big Gulp full of Coke. He sat on the corner by the propane cage in the shade and drank it.

Sweat dripped from his hair into his eyes despite the icy cold soda. How hot was it in the bunker? Or was it cool since it was underground?

Was she strong enough to be there with Steve was what he really wanted to ponder. But somehow, he didn't quite get there. It flitted around his mind, only swimming up to the surface occasionally, much like the words drifting up from the visual garbage on the book's pages.

His father had chosen family over her. Now she was here to bring family to Ben. Was that full circle? A family curse? Luck or doom?

He didn't know.

Finally, the drink was gone, he'd stopped the heavy sweating and the sun had shifted. It was nearly lunchtime.

Ben went back.

The book was waiting for him.

It sat atop the bunker door in a small drift of leaves and small branches.

He picked it up, flipping through it without focusing on any of it for too long. It was pristine. She was there in the book. Back turned to him. Hunched. Like someone protecting something. Their food, maybe?

A small spattering of three drops of blood were on the cover.

Something told him they'd be gone by the time he got home.

She was stronger now. Almost strong enough.

Strong enough for what?

(I don't know)

He put the book in the bag. He was about to hitch it up on his shoulder when curiosity got the better of him and he opened the bunker door.

A smattering of clothes strewn about. The shirt shredded. A small smear of blood she must have missed at the bottom of the left wall. A few small gray stones that he was sure now were Steve's fillings.

Not much else.

Just sneakers and a sports watch and a crumpled water bottle.

There was all the debris of Steve's that had been here when they'd first arrived, but it only proved he'd hung out here once upon a time.

There was nothing to indicate he'd died here. Maybe that he'd gotten naked, but nothing more. Unless the fillings were an issue. But unlike teeth, he imagined it would be very hard to figure out one filling from another.

Ben let the lid slam shut and then he put the rocks atop it, some leaves and branches.

He found his homemade spear and unwrapped the handle of the diving knife until it fell away in his hands. He put that in his backpack and then took the wooden pole and snapped it with his foot. He threw one half one way, and the other half the other.

The surrounding overgrowth of vegetations swallowed each up with a gulp.

Ben headed home. He was hungry again.

CHAPTER 28

AFTER DIGGING in the dregs of the pantry, he made himself a can of SpaghettiOs and opened a can of peaches in fruit juice. His mother—when sober—was always on about added sugar in fruit.

He heated the pasta and ate at the breakfast bar. Ben kept his gaze intently on his food because when he looked up, at times, figures were swirling in the shadows around the edges of the room.

It was very hot outside, 99 and climbing, and he kept the blinds drawn against the sun the way his father had always done. The less sun that got in, the less the AC had to work.

"You listen well."

He looked up to see his dad grinning from the other side of the bar.

He looked very *very* real.

"I tried."

His father nodded. "I know. And you always did very well."

"Are you real?"

Andrew shrugged. "As real as I've ever felt."

"Is she here to bring you back?"

"She's here because you found the book and started to give her offerings. She responds to gifts."

"What gifts did you give her?" Ben asked, afraid of the answer.

His father regarded him for a moment. *Can hallucinations regard you*, Ben wondered.

"Similar to your early gifts. A flap of skin here, a toenail there, a girl's menstrual pad in one case."

"How did you get rid of her?"

"I didn't. I met your mother and had to decide. My own family wasn't great. I saw potential. But then I had a chance…" The specter petered off. Then he shrugged and said, "Something in me chose your mom. Which in the end, chose you."

"Smart," Ben said.

"Or lucky? I don't know," his dad said.

What did he want? A chance with Alice? To see his dad every day like he used to? A protector? Someone who put him first?

A family.

Not one that broke apart as easily as spiderwebs under a clumsy swinging hand. But a family. A unit.

Not a drunken conversation at midnight interrupted by a loud oafish Patrick wearing stained boxer shorts and smoking a cigarette. Not a fight overheard from the upstairs bathroom where they took swings at each other.

Not sneaking into the garage just to smell the smell of his father.

Not going down in the basement to his stuff only to be lectured by his mother who then sobbed and retreated into herself for hours or even days.

Not what he had now.

Maybe what he'd had before.

Maybe something better?

"You in there, son?"

"Yeah. Too far in here. I was just thinking."

"About?"

"About what I want."

"Well, I'll give you a little bit of information and then you keep thinking."

"What's that?" He finished his can of soda and crumpled it to hear the aluminum complain.

"She only needs one more. She's very strong. Almost strong enough to not need your assistance."

A get out of murder free card.

Just one more.

"Thanks for the info, Dad."

His dad chuckled, but when Ben looked up, smiling to himself, his father was gone.

His long-forgotten cell phone burbled with a text.

It displayed a flurry of social media notifications, an app update notice, and a voicemail from his mother.

He read the text first.

Kismet?

Dumb luck?

Either way, it was from Mikey and it read: Want to go exploring today? It's hot but we can go into the woods. Hit me up.

He immediately answered: Sure. Meet me at my house.

Mikey: Can't! I have to do chores until I can sneak out. Wait for me down by the park and I'll sneak out as soon as I can.

Not so easy, maybe.

But he'd figure a way to get him back here. No problem.

He tapped out: I'll text you when I'm there.

Then he listened to the message from his mother. He dreaded it even as he hit the play icon.

Hi baby. I miss you…I'll be home soon. Real soon. I'm trying to clear my head. It's that time of year. I keep thinking about daddy. We met in the summer. But I'll be home soon and we can talk. I love you very much. I'll be home soon…

She kept saying it. Was she trying to convince him or herself?

She was drunk when she left the message that was for sure.

She might want to just stay gone, he thought.

Despite being too young to legally live alone or run a household, he pretty much did it all on his own. He could fake it. He could find a way to fly under the radar.

He grabbed a bottle of water and then his bike. Pedaling to the park slowly, Ben wondering about Mikey and what it would take to get him back to his house.

CHAPTER 29

As IT TURNED OUT, it took nothing more than: "I have some weed at home. Any interest?"

This was said as they wandered aimlessly through the woods. Bugs buzzed them incessantly drawn by sweat and scent.

Mikey perked up. "Yeah? I didn't take you for a smoker."

Ben shrugged. "Once in a while."

It wasn't a lie. Somewhere in the back of his dresser under the paper liner his mother insisted on when he was a kid, was a small bag of weed. It had smelled at first. And he worried she'd find it.

But by then, her days of laundering his clothes and putting them away were long gone. He did his clothes when he ran out and he did hers too, occasionally.

It had lost its smell, and possibly its potency. But it was worth a shot.

And lo and behold, it worked.

"Think you can grab your bike from your house?"

"Nah. They'll see me."

Ben realized it was probably for the best. This way there'd be no disposing of the bike. No explaining it if it was found. It would be right where it always was. At Mikey's house.

"You can ride on the back of mine," he said.

The sun had lowered in the sky. The heat had lessened slightly. He pedaled fast and they flew down the streets—a blur. He didn't want anyone to see them together.

At the house he entered, pausing at the door as if to get a sense of the house. The occupancy.

Like earlier it felt occupied, but not really.

Just the sensation of some presence. Or two.

"Where's this green?"

"In my room."

"You trying to get me naked?" Mikey said, cocking his hip and batting his eyelashes.

Ben was caught off guard. He laughed. "Hardly. Sorry, Mikey. You're not my type."

"Your type has a snatch?"

"Um…not a great way of saying it, but accurate, I guess."

Mikey shrugged. "I'm betting you didn't know until just now that I'm gay." He looked a bit unsure.

Ben checked the AC. Turned it down another degree to fight the heat baking the small house. "Nope. And I don't care to be honest. You can be whatever you want. Date whoever you want. As long as it's not Alice Day."

"Ah ha!" Mikey said.

"Ah ha, what?"

Ben wished Mikey would stop talking and making him laugh. It made him feel a million times worse for what he was about to do. But not as bad as he would have felt once upon a time.

Family came first.

The thought came unbidden and surprising. But he nodded, agreeing with his internal monologue.

"I knew you liked her. I saw you staring at her in the hallway. Like, all the time, man. Like super *obvious*. You have no game, my friend."

Ben shook his head. He was grinning though. "Sit your ass down. I'll go get the weed."

He took the steps two at a time. Worry gnawed at him. What if this went wrong? What if he got caught? What if Mikey escaped?

But this wasn't him playing serial killer. This wasn't a corporeal crime, was it? She was something…other. More. Beyond.

He dug around, his heart kicking when he thought he couldn't find it. Then his fingertip grazed the edge of the plastic bag and he snagged it.

He pulled it out. It was crunchy in the bag. Probably stale.

He sniffed the baggie and smelled mostly plastic, a little bit of funk under it.

He dug around in his nightstand until he found the small glass piece he'd used to smoke the two whole times he'd done it. It had never done much for him, so he'd left it by the wayside.

Mikey was lounging on the sofa with a horror movie streaming when he returned.

"Want a soda?"

"Got any beer?"

Ben had to think. "Maybe? I'll check."

He handed over the weed and the pipe and went to rummage for beer in the garage. As luck would have it, he also found soda.

When he came back, Mikey was laughing. "What kind of sad ass shit is this?"

Ben laughed. "Old."

"I'll say." Mikey dug around in his back pocket and finally came up with a tobacco pouch. "Luckily, I have better taste than you. This shit will mellow us out big time."

He proceeded to roll a pristine joint.

Ben handed over a beer and cracked a soda for himself.

He dropped to the sofa as Mikey lit the joint.

They sat and watched a slasher cutting kids to ribbons. Ben made sure to take only small hits of the pot. He was a lightweight and he knew it.

He also knew, deep down in the center of him where the truth lived, that he wanted to be alert when the time came.

This time he wanted to see.

He sipped his soda and watched Mikey get blissfully wasted.

That was good. It would be easier.

The movie ended and a new one rolled. Mikey's head lolled. He talked about his shitty parents, and the bullies at school, and the fact that he had a mad crush on Greg Anderson.

"Straight as an arrow, mind you, and that's the guy that really gets my dick hard. Not the five twinks who follow me around all the time."

"Sorry, man."

Mikey shrugged. "What are you going to do, right?"

Ben's eyes grew wide as she slid from the shadows. One moment she was one with them, the next she stepped free. Nearly solid. Already, terrifying with her silver eyes, her hectic hair. The teeth that peeked out of her mouth but then disappeared.

Her horns swayed as she advanced. It was like she was dancing to music only she could hear.

Maybe she was.

She seemed to expand and shrink like smoke moving in a soft wind. Her mouth gaping wide, wide like a fisherman's net, then narrowing down to nearly a proboscis.

Ben watched mesmerized. He had the same feeling he experienced watching the manta rays and the sharks at the aquarium. There was such a calm and utter presence about her.

She moved like a predator. Assured and silent.

Mikey made a joke about the movie. Laughed himself silly. But Ben didn't hear.

He watched her. Floating—drifting—rolling toward him like a fog.

And then she was on him. Surrounding him was more like it. For just a second. Her encapsulation of Mikey seemed to stun him. He went silent and panicked.

And then she used her horns. Dipping her head, driving it up, opening her mouth in a silent scream that he somehow felt and heard though no sound was emitted.

She lifted Mikey tall and tossed him. He hit the wall with a thud. Leaving a line of blood trailing down the sunshiney yellow walls.

"Shit," Ben muttered. That would take a lot of cleaning up.

"Don't worry about it. She'll take care of it," his father said from somewhere.

So, he watched. Watched her play with him. Watched her bend him and break him. Watched her lap at him with her long darting tongue. And then finally—mercilessly—watched her devour him.

At four in the morning Ben woke in his room alone and still damp from a shower. He smelled like Men's All in One Shampoo and body wash and his teeth were minty.

He vaguely remembered a river of vomit, a ringing in his ears, soft murmurings that were not quite in English, and hands propelling him upstairs to care for him.

Whose hands he couldn't say, beyond the fact that they certainly weren't Mikey's.

CHAPTER 30

HE WOKE to a knock on the door. He laid there, willing it to go away. If it was Steve's sister again, he couldn't help her.

Finally, when it didn't stop, he got up and found his gym shorts. He didn't bother with a shirt this time. He simply ran a hand through his hair and staggered downstairs.

At the bottom of the steps, he stopped to examine the wall that had been spotted with blood the night before.

Clean as a whistle.

Another knock. The bong of the doorbell.

"Jesus fucking Christ," he muttered. "I'm coming!"

He opened the door to Miss Molly wringing her hands.

She took a step back at his appearance.

"My goodness, Ben, are you okay?"

He looked down at himself, suddenly worried he was somehow covered in gore from Mikey's demise.

Nope. All clean.

"Yeah, I was just asleep. You woke me. Sorry."

"Ah. I apologize. I just wanted to check in. I still haven't seen your mom. Are you okay? Is she coming home soon?"

He thought of the voicemail. He thought of the protector eating his friend. He thought of his father. There were parental forces here, he thought. Then he giggled.

Miss Molly grimaced.

"Sorry, sorry. I'm still half asleep," he said. "She called yesterday. She'll be home today. Tomorrow at the latest," he lied, because his mom hadn't given a distinct time frame. And he wouldn't trust her if she had.

"Oh. Good, then. I was starting to wonder if I should call Child Protective Services."

Cold water trailed down his spine and he smiled his best smile. "No need. I'm fine. I'm on my own a lot. Going to be seventeen soon, Miss Molly. I can even feed myself. I know how to open cans and work a microwave," he teased.

And pay the bills and fix things because my mother was half in the bag all the time…

He didn't say that part.

"Oh, I know. But I do worry. And even if you can take care of yourself, I think there's responsibility there. Your mother should be around for you. You should haven't to fend for yourself." She caught herself and smiled. "Your mother has had a…*hard time* since your father died. I just want to know you're taken care of, Ben. Your dad and I were good friends. At least, I like to think so. I know I've told you that before, but it's true."

They had been. And suddenly saw her worry and her sadness for what it was.

"Trust me. I'm taken care of. And she'll be home soon. I think this trip might have helped her, even," he lied again.

No doubt taking that as possibly a return from rehab, Miss Molly brightened. "Excellent! Well, in the meantime, let me know if you need anything."

When he shut the door, he exhaled so loud and so long he sounded like he was deflating.

He drank a big ass mug of coffee with sugar and non-dairy creamer and wandered through the house.

Things looked pristine. Things looked put together.

The place where parts of Mikey had been strewn across the wall was completely clean. No remains to be found but for some pot on the living room table.

He put it all in a Ziploc bag from the kitchen and hid it in the basement behind a row of books.

He might need it later.

The antler bowl was still there but looking a bit more like an eccentric work of art than a sacrificial receptacle.

He sat down with the mug, listening. All he could hear was the sound of bugs ratcheting up outside. Screeching in the summer heat.

"Did I imagine all this? Was it a dream?" He knew it wasn't. He knew that in his bones, but he couldn't help but think that if this were a book or a movie, that might be how the writer explained it all away.

"Not a dream!"

It was his father's voice. From the workroom. Always his favorite place to putter around.

He went in, not feeling any fear or even any concern. He leaned against the doorway.

"So, what is it?"

His father shrugged, rubbing dirt on a t-shirt with his fingertips. Which was strange. But he knew about strange after the last week

"A new chance? A new life? Maybe think of it as an alternate timeline," he said.

"If you stayed with her and I was your son?"

"Maybe. Or if I was dead and she became real and you formed a family."

"It feels like a really weird Twilight Zone."

"So does life," his father said. He picked at the tee with a safety pin, meticulously creating a hole. "If you told me that I'd die at 42 from melanoma, I'd have laughed at you. If you told me that I, the palest man in existence, would even *get* melanoma I'd have laughed at you."

"What are you doing?" Ben asked, finally. His coffee was done and he was starving.

"Set dressing," his father said.

"I'm going to go eat."

"Go eat. You're a growing boy."

"Do you even eat, Dad? Do I make you some breakfast?"

His father shook his head. "I eat. But not food. Go on now, eat. I'm finishing up. And she's resting up. For later."

"Later?"

"You'll find out. Go."

Ben went.

After he ate and took a shower, he found the tee on his bed. The one his father had been distressing. Set dressing, he'd said.

He could only assume he was supposed to wear it. He had no idea why, but asking too many questions was exhausting. So he put it on. It would make sense later, no doubt.

He didn't bother to question how a dead man had brought him a change of clothes any more than he'd questioned how his father had fashioned him a spear.

It simply happened.

CHAPTER 31

BEN WAS CLEANING up the kitchen that had been dirty way too long when he heard the front door.

He froze.

No one but his mother, Patrick, maybe Miss Molly, and himself had a key. Well, that was a lie. His grandmother did but she lived in Kentucky, so he doubted it was her.

The sound of a bag hitting the floor by the front door. The way it did when his mother would get home from shopping.

His heart kicked. He didn't know how to feel. Good? Bad? Worried?

"Mom?" he said it softly. No way she heard.

There was the sound of the floor creaking from her heavy footsteps even with the AC unit hissing air.

He could feel his thumping pulse at the base of his neck. He felt almost sick with it.

"Ben?" she called out softly as if afraid.

He didn't answer. He found that he couldn't.

His ears filled with pressure like he was slowly climbing in altitude. A wave of vertigo hit him, and he clutched the edge of the counter to steady himself.

She was moving so slowly. Could she feel the weirdness in the house? The surreal feel of it? Or was she just worried about a poor reception?

Ben waited.

She came through the kitchen door blinking like there was too much light in the house. His mother. Short with black hair and green eyes and a stunned expression.

She was beautiful when she wasn't blitzed. Funny when she wasn't shit-faced. Smart when she let herself be. She'd willingly jumped into an open bottle the moment his father died—dealing with her grief in an oblivious kind of way. Not caring that her son was floundering on his own to cope.

There was a wickedly sharp stab of hatred for her. It coursed through him like electricity.

At that moment, behind his mother, in the shadow of the doorway she'd passed through, he caught the sway of antlers. The flash of shining silver eyes. A smooth motion of a jaw unhinging and needle teeth.

"Mom!" he said.

The image faded.

His mother clutched her chest as she studied him. "Ben. Benny! You look—" She took him in and her eyes widened. "Are you okay? You're dirty. You're a mess."

But he wasn't. He was freshly showered and currently cleaning the kitchen.

But her eyes, her wide, bloodshot eyes traveled his messy tee as if it were a map of terrible terrain.

She touched the dirt. Plucked at the hole. She chewed her lower lip, mumbled to herself, looked utterly upset.

He wanted to laugh right in her face. *This* is what upset her? This? A dirty fucking t-shirt?

Not Patrick the terrible? His horrible way with Ben? His foul language, nastiness, drunkenness, brutality. How the asshole had once fucked her with the bedroom door open when he knew damn well that Ben was home and she was way too drunk to comprehend?

This was what upset her.

There it came again. A hot and putrid gush of loathing. He saw himself grabbing her throat. Squeezing. Squeezing until the air came out of her tiny body and her eyes grew aware and she finally— finally!—SAW HIM! Really saw him. And his pain and his need and his god damn loneliness.

In his peripheral vision, a tossing of horns. A flash of hungry metallic eyes. A gnashing of teeth.

If she saw it, his mother didn't react.

He stepped back fast as if he had actually been touching her. His hands on her neck.

"What are you doing here?" He knew the answer, but the words came out anyway. He turned his head toward the protector. The *mother*. Not the Ma or the Mom or the Mommy.

The MOTHER.

He saw it now. Clearly. And he wondered why he hadn't fully seen it before.

She gave you what you needed. And he'd needed her.

"I told you I was coming back."

"Yeah, but—"

"Didn't you believe me?" Her hands strayed all over him, reminding him of wandering overgrown spiders. She plucked and smoothed and patted and cooed.

Bile rose in his throat, liquid fury.

"I...no," he finally said, batting her hands away. "I didn't."

"Have you eaten? Are you okay?"

He stepped back and stared at her. "Do you care?" He pinned her with his gaze, crossed his arms against her seeking hands.

She leveled a gaze at him.

She looked fairly sober, he thought.

Maybe?

Her eyes teared up and his first thought was, too little, too late.

"I know I've been a bad mother—" she started.

"You haven't been a mother at all," he said. "Not for a long time."

Her lips hardened into a tight line. She straightened her spine.

Was she angry? Was she fucking *offended*?

A nasty bark of laugher burst out of Ben so fast he tried to clamp a hand to his mouth to keep it in. He failed. It wiggled through his fingers, issued forth, filled the small sunny kitchen with the antithesis of mirth.

"Benjamin!"

She was, he realized. She was fucking offended.

More laughter. So big and so loud it hurt his ears to hear. And all the while, in the corners of the room—in the shadows and the gloom —he could see her circling.

His real mother now.

"Are you actually shocked? Are you actually hurt?" he asked between great whooping coughs of laughter.

She crossed her arms.

"I've done my best."

"That's funny," he said.

"Are you high?" she asked suddenly, coming toward him, hands out. An ah-ha look on her face as if she's cracked the code.

"Would you know? Are you sober enough to deduce that?"

Anger—real anger—flared in her green eyes. She looked enraged.

"You should be humbled that I'd even talk to you," he said, his voice dipping low.

That gave her pause. He wasn't yelling. He was good and truly angry, and he was getting quieter. The gathering storm of everything he'd held in for all this time was swirling into a jagged black eye of menace.

"Of course I would notice," she stammered. He'd never spoken to her like this. She didn't know what to do. "And why wouldn't you talk to me?"

"Because you took off with your piece of shit boyfriend."

"I had some things to figure out."

"Like if you were going to come back? Be a mother? Have a son?" Spit flew from his lips. He could feel himself losing control of his emotions, and for the first time he could recall—he didn't care.

"I'm always your mother," she said. Tears streamed down her face and it only made him angrier.

He shook his head. Backed away.

The sinewy dark shape of a shark-like predator circling the perimeter was there. He could see it. He relished it. Welcomed it. Wanted it. It was what he needed. What he deserved as a son. As someone who'd suffered loss, too.

"I lost both of my parents when dad died," he said. He said it so softly that even he had trouble hearing his voice.

She gasped. Said it, again, "I am always your mother, Ben."

"You haven't been a mother since he died. You've been a drunk. You've been absent. You've been self-centered, out of touch. You've been a whore. But you haven't been a mother," he said.

It came rushing out of him like an infection. When just enough pressure is applied to a wound and the body relents and releases. A thick putrid rush of everything he'd been holding in since his father died.

It all spewed out of him.

He watched her face change and his words sink in. It was almost as if time slowed. The world wobbled and things grew shaky.

She said something he didn't quite hear. Maybe *watch your mouth* or *show some respect*, both favorites of hers from his growing up years.

Either way, he didn't hear it. He simply saw the blur of her hand as it shot out and heard the immense dead wood snap of her palm striking his cheek. His head rocked, his ear muffled like a microphone banged against a hard surface, and his teeth snapped together so hard he heard the rock hard crunch inside his skull.

And then she was screaming.

Screaming at him. Screaming for him. Screaming a gurgling wet scream that grew lower and lower like meat in a garbage disposal as it churned.

He saw the needle teeth close around his mother's tiny white neck. The dry brush in a high wind swirl of hair, the antlers bouncing with every scissoring motion of the jaws.

He saw his mother's blood as red as his favorite crayon in kindergarten. He heard the snap of bone and the wet eating sounds and the whish whish whish of her feet trying to touch the kitchen floor but only the very top of the toes of her sandals touched.

Then he heard his name.

"Ben? Ben?" He turned toward the dim living room. The house buttoned up tight against the unforgiving summer sun and heat welcomed shadows and pockets of dark.

His father.

"Ben come in here and let mother eat."

He went. His legs numb, his ears ringing, his heart pounding. His fingertips felt a million miles away and he wondered if he was in shock. He brushed a hand across his face because it tickled, and his fingers came back tainted with blood.

"Lie down. It will be okay," his father said.

He did what he was told. He remembered his father tucking him in for naps when he was little, or bundling him up on the sofa when he had a bad cold or the flu, or putting him to bed at night with a funny fairy tale, half as it was written and half ad-libbed.

Lying down as his father stood near him talking softly—nonsense sounds, burbling like water over rocks—as familiar and comforting as chicken soup or hot chocolate.

He stayed there in the dim, wondering if this was all real. If he'd snapped. Was he sitting somewhere catatonic? Or worse, was he in the kitchen killing his mother, this whole family thing a perverse but vivid fantasy that propelled him, the killing machine?

A sob hitched his throat, but his father said something else. Softly. More tone than words.

And Ben let himself doze.

It was a weird half-awake, half-asleep thing. A limbo. A place to hide as the mother finished her meal.

CHAPTER 32

THE IMAGE WAS SURREAL. He woke to them standing over him. His father, looking down the way his father always had. The mother, in the peripheral but not as much as she once had been.

The stronger she became did she become more visible, he wondered. Or just to him?

"It's all done," his father said. "She took care of it. It's all clean and all is well."

He could smell tobacco. His father's. Did he become more and more corporeal as well?

Ben's head felt hollow, his ears rang.

He sat up and his body felt heavy and light all at once.

"Family is everything," his father said.

"Family is everything," Ben echoed.

The house did not have that empty feeling. He didn't feel untethered and alone.

"There's just one more thing," his father said, sitting down on the sofa next to him.

"What's that?"

The hair on the back of his neck prickled and he worried about the answer.

"It's something I can't do," his father said.

She was there, hovering behind him. Leaning close. Warming his back with her presence.

It was terrifying and pleasant all at once.

"Families get better every time they expand. The larger the pack, the safer you are."

Ben stared at his dad. He looked as real as he had the day he died.

Was he talking about bringing someone in from the outside, or the more obvious solution?

His mouth was suddenly dry. His skin suddenly too tight.

"Okay," he said.

"It won't take much," his father said. "It will be about as intense as drawing blood. However, it does, have to be done the original way," he said, laughing. "We aren't equipped for in vitro fertilization in this joint."

His dad winked at him even as Ben's stomach dropped.

But family was everything. He'd learned that all too well when he'd lost his. And now, now he had another chance. This family didn't seem like it would leave.

It was down by the antler bowl that his dad led him. A straw mat on the hard concrete floor. He laid down, feeling about as relaxed as someone in the electric chair.

"Relax," his father said. "The best you can. This is good. Another family member. An innocent for the mother to look after. A young one for you to help raise. Giving your love and your knowledge is the most important thing there is."

Ben listened to it all. Nodded. He was a bizarre mix of calm and horrified. He laid there, heart pounding.

He could see her circling in the shadows. Coalescing, fading out, coming together again. It seemed no matter how tangible she became, that ability stayed with her.

What a wonderful predator she was.

"I won't watch," his father reassured him. "I'll go in the work-room. And it won't take long. I assure you. I never got this far—to this point, but I imagine it isn't long."

Ben willed him away. He wanted his father to go and to shut his eyes and to do what he had to do for his family.

She came toward him in the dim light. She circled and swirled. Was it a mating dance or a safety check? Was this a ritual and he was at the center of it?

He didn't know. But he did know that the closer the mother came, the calmer he felt. A sticky slow warming of his body. A fuzzy charming white static in his head.

She settled on him eventually, in a way no mother ever should.

Ben was vaguely aware the way he was aware when he dozed on the sofa with the TV on. He could hear the rustling of her. Her hair, her horns, her gowns.

The sensation of being enveloped. Not in a welcoming warmth the way it had been with Alice. That was bliss. Honeyed warmth all around him, inside and out.

This was like being taken into a cool black hole. There was a cave-like chill to it and he tried not to recognize it. Kept his eyes shut and his mind loose.

It was over quick enough. Like an extraction more than a release.

She was gone and he was there, splayed out on the ground. Exhausted and cold, he slept.

When he woke in the dark of the night, there was an ancient afghan draped over him.

He got up, body stiff, and stumbled to bed.

In the dark of the upstairs hall, he saw the spare bedroom door was open. He glanced in. She was in there, standing in the dark corner of the room, silver eyes glinting, patting and rubbing.

Her belly had swollen already.

How quickly would this brother/son be born? And how did he know it would be a boy?

Ben went to bed and slept the way only exhausted broken people can.

This was all terribly odd and wrong, and yet, he was comforted.

He slept without dreaming.

Humming could be heard from the room next door.

CHAPTER 33

IT WASN'T the smell of bacon or the sound of a radio that woke him. What woke him was the sound of his father's whistling from somewhere in the house.

When he strained to hear, he heard slithery, dry thumps from the room next door.

The nursery

He made coffee and a piece of toast. He looked at the sunshine through the floral curtains.

In the kitchen sink was a small gray rock.

Not a rock, he saw. A filling. One of his mom's, no doubt. The mother had missed something.

Ben stuck the filling in his pocket.

A memento.

The doorbell rang and he exhaled slowly. Who would it be this time?

What kind of thrall did the mother hold over outsiders? Was he safe? Would he have to kill again? To keep their secret?

Questions and worries rolled through his mind as he dragged himself toward the front door.

He had a stab of panic wondering if it would be a police officer, there to arrest him for killing Steve or luring Mikey to his death or maybe PETA here to get him for not saving Solace or—

He looked through the peephole and saw Alice. Lovely Alice in a white tank top and jeans shorts. He hair in twin braids, her smile untainted. Someone who had never killed. Someone who would never guess he had.

"Hey, there!" she said when he opened the door. "How's stuff go—"

She tried to step in and he blocked her with his body.

Her face fell. Wondering if he'd lost interest? Wondering if he'd gotten what he wanted from her and was done?

She had no idea it was a protective gesture.

"Sorry," he said, smiling down at her. "Can I meet you in a bit? At your place? Or the park? Mother is here and we're settling something. She's weird about people in the house."

She looked and did indeed see his mother's returned car.

She looked hurt and he caught on to what she might think. Black people in the house.

He put his hand on her arm and said softly, "All people, Alice. Anyone. No one is welcome in my house by my dumbass mother."

Relief spread over her face, knowing it wasn't her. Knowing they were okay. "Sure. We can meet. An hour? Or you need more time?"

"No that's good," he said. "Your place or the park?"

She smiled. "Come to my house. We can watch a movie. Maybe something scary. My folks are at a cookout."

"Sounds great," he said. "I love scary things. The scarier the better."

She kissed him quickly and warmth spread through him. Hope. Affection. He wanted her safe. Wanted her far far away from his new family life.

He trusted the mother to have his back, but not to keep away from Alice.

He'd waited too long for her. Thought it would never happen. Now it had.

Ben didn't know what the near future held for his new family, but he planned to keep Alice *far* away from it. She would not be one of the sacrifices to the mother.

The thought rose, bitter and unwelcome:

At least for now.

ACKNOWLEDGMENTS

Thanks to Jason. Always to Jason. He's my cheerleader, proofreader, the person I bounce endless ideas off of, my best friend, and my partner. And thanks, of course, to Sam Richard who read a whole other novella before we got to this one and then decided to give my weird little book a home. I figured this would be the one to wander the desert for years before finding a place to live. I was wrong!

ABOUT THE AUTHOR

For the last 15+ years, Ali Seay has written professionally under a pen name. Now she's shaken off her disguise to write as herself in the genre she loves the most. Ali lives in Baltimore with her family. Her greatest desire is to own a vintage Airstream and hit the road. Her novella *Go Down Hard* was released in 2020 by Grindhouse Press. For more information visit aliseay.com or find her on Twitter @Ali-Seay11 or Instagram @introvert_fitness

CONTENT WARNING

Contains graphic violence, alcoholism, harm to animals, death, and sex.

ALSO FROM WEIRDPUNK BOOKS

Things Have Gotten Worse Since We Last Spoke by Eric LaRocca

Sadomasochism. Obsession. Death.

A whirlpool of darkness churns at the heart of a macabre ballet between two lonely young women in an internet chat room in the early 2000s--a darkness that threatens to forever transform them once they finally succumb to their most horrific desires.

What have you done today to deserve your eyes?

"A startling affair...I'll be cleaning up particles of darkness in my office for weeks."

— JOSH MALERMAN (*BIRD BOX, INSPECTION*)

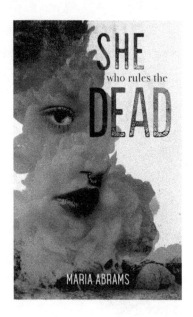

Henry has received a message: he needs to sacrifice five people to the demon that's been talking to him in his nightmares. He already has four, and number five, Claire, is currently bound in the back of his van.

Too bad Claire isn't exactly human.

"I fucking loved this book! Just when I thought I knew where it was headed--I was wrong. And I love to be wrong. A thrilling ride. I want more!"

— Ali Seay (*Go Down Hard*)

Beautiful/Grotesque - Edited by Sam Richard

Five authors of strange fiction, Roland Blackburn (*Seventeen Names For Skin*), Jo Quenell (*The Mud Ballad*), Katy Michelle Quinn (*Girl in the Walls*), Joanna Koch (*The Wingspan of Severed Hands*), and Sam Richard (*Sabbath of the Fox-Devils*) each bring you their own unique vision of the macabre and the glorious violently colliding. From full-on hardcore horror, to decadently surreal nightmares, and noir-fueled psychosis, to an eerie meditation on grief, and familial quiet horror, *Beautiful/Grotesque* guides us through the murky waters where the monstrous and the breathtaking meet.

They are all beautiful. They are all grotesque.

CPSIA information can be obtained
at www.ICGtesting.com
Printed in the USA
BVHW071225210821
614139BV00002B/11